Book Nine

EPIC ZERO 9

Tales of a Souled-Out Superhero

By

R.L. Ullman

But That's Another Story... Press

Cover design and character illustrations by Yusup Mediyan.

Published by But That's Another Story… Press
Ridgefield, CT

Printed in the United States of America.

First Printing, 2021.

ISBN: 978-1-953713-08-7
Library of Congress Control Number: 2021910259

For Matthew,
here it is!

BOOKS BY R.L. ULLMAN

EPIC ZERO SERIES

EPIC ZERO:
Tales of a Not-So-Super 6th Grader

EPIC ZERO 2:
Tales of a Pathetic Power Failure

EPIC ZERO 3:
Tales of a Super Lame Last Hope

EPIC ZERO 4:
Tales of a Total Waste of Time

EPIC ZERO 5:
Tales of an Unlikely Kid Outlaw

EPIC ZERO 6:
Tales of a Major Meta Disaster

EPIC ZERO 7:
Tales of a Long Lost Leader

EPIC ZERO 8:
Tales of a Colossal Boy Blunder

EPIC ZERO 9:
Tales of a Souled-Out Superhero

MONSTER PROBLEMS SERIES

MONSTER PROBLEMS:
Vampire Misfire

MONSTER PROBLEMS 2:
Down for the Count

MONSTER PROBLEMS 3:
Prince of Dorkness

TABLE OF CONTENTS

ONE

I BOWL A GUTTER BALL

It feels great to be in my costume again.

Trust me when I tell you there's only so much TV a kid can watch, especially when the shows keep getting interrupted by Meta Monitor alerts. Thankfully, now that my ribs are fully healed, I'm back in business!

So, look out creeps!

And speaking of creeps, there's plenty of them around after the whole Meta-Man fiasco. That alien psycho demolished Lockdown in his search for Max Mayhem, freeing hundreds of dangerous Meta villains. We finally stopped him with the help of the Protectors of the Planet, but not before he fractured three of my ribs. Honestly, I would have happily fractured *all* of my ribs if it meant getting rid of that monster.

The good news is that the Freedom Force recaptured most of the escapees, but a few of them are still on the loose. That's why Dad and I are here.

We're standing outside a large, rundown warehouse on the outskirts of town. With its boarded-up windows and tinted glass door, you'd think it was empty inside. But we know better because we traced one of the Lockdown fugitives to this exact location. His name is Airstream, a Meta 3 Energy Manipulator who can control air currents.

All we need to do now is reel him in.

The entrance is down a flight of steep, concrete stairs, and there's a tattered sign on the door that reads: *Strike It Rich Bowling. Get Yourself Out of the Gutter. No children allowed.*

Well, that's a first. I don't think I've ever seen a bowling alley that banned kids before. But Dad said I shouldn't be surprised. After all, this is no ordinary bowling alley—it's a secret meeting place for bad guys.

"Put this on," Dad says, handing me a tan trench coat and matching fedora hat. "This place is full of shady characters. If anyone recognizes us there could be trouble. Tuck your cape inside your belt so it doesn't flare out and let me do all the talking. The last thing we need is for someone to notice you're just a kid."

"Got it," I say, putting on the coat and hat. "And mum's the word." I pretend to lock my mouth shut and throw away the key.

"Great," Dad says, putting on his own hat and coat.

"Now let's go in there and grab Airstream."

I nod in agreement, but as soon as I take my first step down the steep stairs, I hesitate. For some reason, I feel uneasy. I mean, I know I'm rusty and all, but I don't think that's it. It's only when I see Dad standing by the door that it hits me.

The entrance is way below ground.

Suddenly, I flash back to all of my other underground missions. Like the time I chased Alligazer into the sewer system. Or when I dropped into the 13th Dimension with Aries to rescue Wind Walker. I don't know why, but underground missions and I just don't mix.

"Are you okay?" Dad asks. "Do you want to wait here outside?"

"N-No," I say, my voice cracking. "I'm good."

I take a deep breath and head down the stairs.

As soon as Dad opens the door my senses go on overload. Between the dim lighting, the CRASH of bowling balls against pins, and the putrid, antiseptic smell, I feel a little disoriented. But I shake it off and follow Dad across the dingy, blue carpet to the front desk where a short, bald man with a long, black beard works the cash register. Behind him are dozens of bowling lanes occupied by rough-looking customers in street clothes.

"Excuse me, sir," Dad says, "we're looking for someone who—"

"Yeah, ain't we all?" the man interjects gruffly. Then, he looks us up and down and says, "You fellas gonna bowl in those getups?"

"Um, no," Dad says. "We're not here to bowl. We're looking for—"

"Look, I don't want no trouble," the man interrupts again, pointing at us with a stubby finger. "I'm not gonna have my joint busted up by masked hooligans like you. If you're here to bowl then bowl. If not, take a hike."

Well, this is going swimmingly.

I take a step back to the exit but Dad just stands there and says, "Give us a lane."

"Good choice," the man says, pushing buttons on his console. "Lane thirteen. Pay when you're done. The wings are half off when you buy a large pitcher of beer."

"Great," Dad says, starting to walk off.

"Hey, hold on there, Superman," the man says, looking down at Dad's feet. "No way you're scuffing up my lanes with those boots. You gotta rent bowling shoes."

"Right," Dad says, removing his red boots and putting them on the counter. "Give me a size fourteen." And then he puts his hand on my shoulder before I can speak and says, "And my partner here needs a size seven. An adult size seven."

"Comin' up," the man says, and then he reaches down and places two pairs of hideous brown-and-green bowling shoes on the counter.

What is it with bowling shoes anyway? Are they made this ugly on purpose so no one steals them? I turn in my boots and take my pair, but as we walk towards our lane I whisper, "Are we really bowling right now?"

"No," Dad whispers back, "but now isn't the time to make a scene. Even though no one's in costume, I already recognize two Meta villains in here. Slime-Wave is on lane four and Cat's Paw is on lane twenty."

I take a seat in our lane and lean back to get a clear view of lane four. That's when I spot a skinny man with greasy, blond hair picking up a neon-green ball. Yep, even without his costume, I recognize Slime-Wave. He's a Meta 1 Energy Manipulator who projects slime from his nose. Then, I lean forward and see a woman to our right with red, spikey hair and super-long fingernails bowling with cat-like quickness. Well, there's no doubt about it, that's Cat's Paw. She's a Meta 2 with Super-Speed.

"Where's Airstream?" I ask.

"I don't know," Dad says, tying his bowling shoes. "Let's split up and do some reconnaissance. I'll go left and you go right. But if you spot him don't do anything without me. Remember, Airstream is extremely dangerous."

"Got it," I say, tightening the way-too-long laces on my bowling shoes. But as soon as I stand up my feet slide on the carpet and I nearly topple over. Awesome. Gotta love the slippery soles of these ridiculous clown shoes.

I head over to the ball rack and pretend to examine some balls while studying the bowlers. Slime-Wave was easy to pick out of a crowd, but Airstream isn't as distinctive. From what I remember from his profile, he has brown hair, brown eyes, and a medium build. But that could describe a million people.

I kneel to look at a purple ball with orange flames when I think I spot him. He's on lane six just about to bowl. I watch him closely, looking for any sign that I've got my man. Then, he releases the ball and it veers sharply left, rolling straight for the gutter. Except, the next thing I know, the man waves his hand and the ball suddenly changes direction landing a perfect strike!

Bingo! That's got to be Airstream!

Wow. I guess villains cheat at everything—including bowling.

I try to get Dad's attention, but he's on the other side of the alley and I don't want to make a scene. I look back at Airstream who is now standing at the ball return looking my way! Uh oh, does he recognize me?

I know Dad told me not to do anything without him, but I'm pretty sure he wouldn't want Airstream to get away. And if I wave or yell to call Dad over it'll definitely tip Airstream off. So, it looks like I need to go solo.

I stand up and head over to his lane.

"Hey, nice strike," I say, stopping on the platform. "But does it really count if you had to use your Meta powers to get it?"

"Who are you?" Airstream asks, looking at me funny.

I couldn't have asked for a better segue. So, I throw off my hat and trench coat and say, "I'm—"

"—Epic Zebra!" comes a deep voice from behind.

Huh? I spin around to find a very large, muscular man staring down at me with a big, goofy smile on his face. And in his giant mitts are three pitchers of beer and three platters of chicken wings.

"You're Epic Zebra," he repeats. "You were on the news a while back."

"Well, yeah, I was," I say, thinking back to my nightmare of an interview on the CNC Morning Newsflash. "But my name isn't really—"

"Didn't you read the sign?" the large man interjects. "No children allowed. This is an adult establishment."

"Well, yes," I say. "But—"

"Hang on," the large man adds, his brow furrowing. "Aren't you a member of the Freedom Force?"

"Well, yes again," I say, standing up a little taller. "As a matter of fact, I am. And I'm here to—"

"Wait, *he's* on the Freedom Force?" Airstream says, cutting me off. "You're kidding, right?"

"Well, no," I say. "And I don't know why you find that so surprising. I might be a kid, but—"

"Scram, kid," the large man says brushing past me and handing Airstream the wings. "Let us bowl in peace. Besides, we've got plans to make."

"The only things you'll be making," comes a voice from behind me, "are your prison beds when we return you to Lockdown."

"Captain Justice!" Airstream says, his eyes bugging

out of his head.

"The one and only," Dad says. "And I see you've met my colleague, Epic Zero." Then, Dad glares at me and whispers, "Who should have stuck to our agreement."

"Sorry," I say sheepishly.

"We'll talk later," Dad whispers. Then, he says to the crooks, "But it's our lucky day because we have our very own two for one special. Not only did we find Airstream, but we've also found another Lockdown escapee. Isn't that right, Pulverizer?"

Pulverizer? That big guy is Pulverizer? No wonder his biceps are bigger than his head. And he's got Meta 2 Super-Strength!

"That's right, Captain," Pulverizer says. "Except, we're not going back to Lockdown. So, let's celebrate. This round is on you!"

The next thing I know, Pulverizer throws the pitchers of beer right in Dad's face. But that's not all, because Airstream flicks his wrists, lifts several bowling balls into the air, and then sends them straight at me!

I duck and they fly over my head, CRASHING through the wall behind me. But when I look back, I see one more! And it's coming so fast I can't avoid it!

UGH! I grunt as it nails me in the left thigh! Ouch, that really hurt! I'm lucky it didn't hit me in the ribs. But as soon as I step towards Airstream my whole leg feels numb and I topple to the ground.

"Epic Zero!" Dad calls out.

"Look out!" I yell as Pulverizer rears back his giant fist. He's gonna pummel Dad!

I focus fast and bathe Pulverizer with my negation power right as his fist connects with Dad's jaw.

CRACK!

"My hand!" Pulverizer screams as he bends over in pain. "Your face broke my hand!"

"Sorry, Pulverizer," Dad says with a wink. "I guess that was a real jaw breaker." And then Dad slugs Pulverizer so hard the villain flies down the lane and SMASHES into the pins, leaving only the two far ones standing.

"I hate those 7-10 splits," Dad says. Then, he turns to Airstream and says, "Care to help me pick up a spare?"

"I'm out of here!" Airstream says, raising his arms and taking off into the air.

"Hey, you didn't pay!" the owner yells as Airstream flies over his head.

I try standing but my leg still feels dead. So, I focus my concentration again and send my negation powers in Airstream's direction. Suddenly, Airstream loses altitude and SMASHES headfirst through the tinted glass door.

He doesn't get back up.

"I knew you guys were trouble!" the owner yells. "You're gonna pay for this!"

Dad collects Pulverizer and when he returns I realize we're surrounded by dozens of other bad guys, including

Slime-Wave and Cat's Paw! I swallow hard. This is about to get ugly—real ugly.

"Our apologies," Dad says, hoisting an unconscious Pulverizer over his shoulder, "but these men are escaped criminals. Now, I'll happily pay for the repairs, but if you're referring to some other kind of payment then I advise everyone to back up before you all end up joining these two at Lockdown."

"Okay, relax, boy scout," the owner says, his hands in the air. "Give them some space!" he yells to the crowd.

"Let's go, Epic Zero," Dad says.

He helps me up and I hobble along behind him when I remember something. I limp over to the front desk, grab our boots, and head for the exit.

"Hey, keep the shoes," the owner says graciously.

"Gee, thanks," I say. "We'll cherish them."

Then, Dad scoops up Airstream with his other arm and we head out in our brand-new bowling shoes.

Meta Profile
The Freedom Force
Captain Justice
Class: Super-Strength
Meta :
Ms. Understood
Class: Psychic
Meta :
Glory Girl
Class: Flight
Meta :
Shadow Hawk
Class: None
Meta :
Epic Zero
Class: Meta Manipulator
Meta :
TechnocRat
Class: Super-Intellect
Meta :
Blue Bolt
Class: Super-Speed
Meta :
Master Mime
Class: Magic
Meta :
Makeshift
Class: Energy Manipulator
Meta :

TWO

I HATE SCARY MOVIES

After we dropped Airstream and Pulverizer at Lockdown, I received my *own* form of punishment.

Dad lectured me the whole ride home about how I should have waited for him before approaching Airstream. I didn't want to hear it, but I knew he was right. And now I'm so sore I can hardly move.

Not only is my left thigh still smarting after getting nailed with that bowling ball, but my ribs are also a little tender. Fortunately, TechnocRat checked me out in the Medi-wing and nothing is broken. But I do have an impressive bowling-ball-sized welt on my thigh to commemorate the occasion, complete with the outlines of three finger holes.

Awesome.

Since we finished late and missed dinner, I decided to raid the Galley cupboard for a bowl of Frosted Letter-Bites cereal. They're shaped like letters of the alphabet and topped with frosting. I know they aren't the healthiest snack in the world, but hey, after a hard day's work sometimes you've gotta treat yourself.

I pour the milk and sit down when I feel something brush my leg under the table. Great, an invisible Dog-Gone is lurking down there, just waiting to strike. I hate it when he's in stealth mode like this. Sometimes I'll forget he's even there, which is exactly what he wants. And if I get up to get something he'll pounce on my food and the beast will feast.

But not this time. This bowl of Frosted Letter-Bites is all mine and I'm gonna savor each bite. I load up my spoon when—

"Does Mom know you're eating that?" comes a snarky, all-too-familiar voice.

"No," I say, lowering my spoon, "she doesn't."

"Well, I don't think she'd approve," Grace says, entering the Galley and leaning against the counter. "In case you forgot, she doesn't like us eating junk like that, especially for dinner. Besides, that's Makeshift's cereal. Did you ask him if you could have some?"

"Well, no," I say, super-annoyed. "But he eats our stuff all the time. I'm sure he won't care."

"There you go again," Grace says, shaking her head.

"Not thinking about the needs or feelings of other people. No wonder your picture is in the dictionary next to the word 'selfish.'"

"*My* picture?" I say, now outraged. "What are you talking about? Unlike you, I think about other people all the time. Weren't you the one who forgot to return TechnocRat's Future Vision goggles?"

"I gave them back," Grace says, buffing her nails. "I just wanted to see what I'd look like in twenty years."

"Well, I'm shocked the goggles didn't break," I say.

"That's it," Grace says, standing up. "I'm telling Mom what you're eating."

"Go for it," I say, lifting my spoon. I just want to take a freaking bite.

"Don't worry," Grace says. "I will."

"You'll what?" Mom asks, rounding the corner with several bags of groceries floating in the air behind her. She lines them up with her mind and places them gently on the counter. Then, she sees me and says, "Elliott, what in the world are you eating?"

"Holy cow!" I say, dropping my spoon. "Can't a kid eat a bowl of cereal around here?"

"Didn't you have dinner?" Mom asks. "I left you a plate of meatloaf in the refrigerator."

"How was I supposed to know that?" I say.

"I always make you a plate if you miss dinner," Mom says, opening the refrigerator. "You know that."

"Well, I forgot, okay?" I say, frustrated. "It's been a

while since I went on a mission, remember?"

"I hear you," Mom says, warming up my plate in the microwave. "But that's not a healthy choice for a growing superhero like you."

Are you kidding me? I'm just trying to eat some cereal, is that so bad? Then, I look down to see a group of Frosted Letter-Bites floating together in the milk spelling the word: N-E-V-E-R.

Well, that's ironic since I'm clearly N-E-V-E-R going to eat this bowl of cereal. Then, the microwave BEEPS and Mom opens it with her mind. Before I can react she mind-lifts my cereal bowl off the table and replaces it with the plate of meatloaf. As my bowl floats away, I see Grace wearing the biggest I-told-you-so smile in the history of humankind.

"Enjoy your meatloaf," Grace says smugly.

"Oh, I will," I say. "Just look out for leftovers in your boots."

"You wouldn't dare!" Grace says.

"I wouldn't be so sure of that," I say.

"Enough bickering, you two," Mom says. "Elliott, you still have homework to do. Please take care of it after dinner."

"C'mon, Mom," I say, "I was out with Dad all afternoon. Can I just do it tomorrow?"

"What's that old saying?" Grace pipes in. "Don't put off until tomorrow what you can do today."

"Really?" I say. "I thought it was 'don't stick your

nose in other people's business.'"

"I said *enough*," Mom says. "But your sister is right, we don't know what might come up tomorrow, so you should do it tonight."

I look at Grace who sticks out her tongue.

Well, it's been a great night. First I'm down a bowl of cereal and now I'm stuck doing algebra problems.

BEEP! BEEP! BEEP!

Speaking of problems.

"What is that noise?" Mom says, looking around.

"It's my Next Gen transmitter watch," I say, looking at my wrist.

<Selfie: Epic, we're watching a scary movie 2-night. Wanna come?>

Yes! Talk about great timing. This might be the get-out-of-jail-free card I was hoping for. Plus, I haven't seen my friends for a while because of my rib injury.

"What's going on?" Grace asks.

But as she tries looking at my watch, I cover the screen. I'd love to tell them I have a mission to go on, but that won't work since Next Gen is still under the watchful eye of the Freedom Force. Plus, Mom's a Psychic so I might as well tell the truth.

"The gang is watching a movie tonight," I say. "Can I go?"

"What kind of a movie?" Grace asks.

"What's the difference?" I say. "And I'm asking Mom, not you."

"Okay, I'll ask then," Mom says. "What kind of a movie is it?"

Drat. "According to Selfie," I say, "it's, um, a scary movie."

"A scary movie?" Grace repeats with a chuckle. "You can't handle scary movies. You'll have nightmares for weeks."

"I will not!" I say. "That was years ago."

"Says the kid who ran out of the room five minutes into Night of the Living Bread," Grace says. "And that was an animated movie!"

"Look, that sourdough was pure evil and you know it!" I say. Then, I turn to Mom and plead, "Can I see my friends, Mom? Please? I mean, I've been stuck here for weeks waiting for my ribs to heal."

Mom stares at me with her I'm-about-to-say-no face, but then she relaxes her expression. "What time will you be back?"

"Seriously?" Grace says. "Are you really letting him go? What about his homework?"

"No later than nine," I say. "I promise."

"Alright," Mom says. "But please finish your meatloaf first. Deal?"

"Deal!" I say.

I text Selfie I'm coming and then stuff my face. When I'm finished, I clear my dish, hug Mom, and then blow Grace a kiss as I skip off to the Hangar.

***

I take a Freedom Ferry to the Hangout and park in the woods behind Selfie's house. I feel kind of bad leaving Dog-Gone behind, but he's pretty much the worst movie companion of all time. He'll settle in nice and quiet, and by the time the previews end, you'll realize he's eaten all of your popcorn. So, tonight I'm going Dog-Gone-free.

Although I didn't want to admit it, Grace is right, I really do hate scary movies. I know they're fake and all, but they completely freak me out. Maybe it's the dumb decisions the characters make, like 'hey, what's that strange noise outside my window at 4 am? I should investigate.' Or maybe it's the creepy background music that always ratchets up right when something bad is going to happen. Whatever it is, scary movies make me anxious.

And don't I have enough anxiety in my life already?

But I'm willing to put myself through this to see my friends. I mean, I haven't seen the team in weeks, so it'll be nice to hang out together—especially with Selfie.

As I approach the treehouse, I hear—

"Hey, Epic! I'm glad you made it."

"Same here," I say, looking up at Selfie who is leaning over the railing. It's really great to see her again, even though my stomach gets butterflies every time I do. I smile and start climbing the ladder.

"Are you okay?" she asks. "It looked like you were

limping across the lawn. Are you sure you're totally healed?"

"Oh, yeah," I say, reaching the platform. "I just got hit in the leg with a bowling ball, that's all. You know, the usual stuff."

"Right," she says. "Well, I guess that answers my second question." Then, she looks down at my feet.

As I follow her gaze, my eyes land on my feet and I feel my face go flush. I can't believe it! I'm still wearing those stupid bowling shoes! Well, that's embarrassing.

"You're making quite the fashion statement," Night Owl says.

"Hey," Skunk Girl says. "I bet if you bowled Pinball, you couldn't miss. You'd get a strike every time."

"Well, aren't you just hilarious," Pinball says, absently rubbing his round tummy. "Can we just watch the movie already? I've got to be home by nine. I have an orthodontist appointment in the morning."

"Okay, everyone chill," Selfie says, rolling over a cart with a TV on it. "Take a seat by the snacks and I'll get this started."

Snacks? I look over and see a table with boxes of popcorn on it. Yep, good thing I didn't bring Dog-Gone.

"Um, what movie are we watching anyway?" I ask as I take a seat on the floor.

"It's called Zombie Buffet," Skunk Girl says enthusiastically. "It's got an awesome tagline."

"Oh, cool," I say. "What is it?"

"You'll never want to eat again," she says dramatically.

"Well, that's appetizing," I say, my voice cracking. "I assume it's animated, right?"

"Animated?" Skunk Girl says, looking at me funny. "No, it's not… Wait a minute, you're not scared, are you?"

"What, me? No way," I say with a way-too-nervous-sounding laugh. "Are you kidding? Me? Scared?"

"Let me squeeze in here," Selfie says, sitting down between me and Skunk Girl.

Great, just what I need. I was hoping to close my eyes through the terrifying parts, but now I'll have to watch the whole thing. The last thing I want is for Selfie to think I'm a complete goober.

"Did everyone get a snack?" Selfie asks, holding up her box of popcorn. "Epic, where's yours?"

I look at the table but all of the boxes are gone. What happened to mine? Then, I hear CRUNCHING behind me, and when I turn I see Pinball stuffing his hands into two boxes at once.

"Hey, you stole my popcorn!" I say.

"I did?" Pinball says. "Oh, sorry. Here." Then, he licks his fingers and offers me one of the boxes.

"Um, no, you keep it," I say.

"Gee, thanks!" Pinball says, munching away.

Just. Freaking. Wonderful.

Now, I not only have to watch the movie, but I get

to hear Pinball scarfing down my popcorn.

Maybe I should have stayed on the Waystation.

"Here, you can share with me," Selfie says, offering me her box.

But then again, maybe not.

"Now, let's get scared out of our minds," Selfie says, clicking the remote control.

Okay, here we go. I take a deep breath and exhale as the title, Zombie Buffet, pops onto the screen. Then comes the creepy background music. I reach into the popcorn box when my hand bumps into Selfie's hand.

"Sorry," I whisper, looking at Selfie.

"It's okay," she whispers back with a smile.

OOOOOOOOOOOOOOOOOOO!

Wow, the volume is really loud. But when I look back at the screen the camera is focused on two people having a peaceful meal in a restaurant. There's not a zombie in sight.

OOOOOOOOOOOOOOOOOOO!

Okay, that was even louder. But this time I was watching the movie and it didn't seem to come from there. I look at the others who are totally engrossed in the movie.

That's weird. Am I the only one who—

Suddenly, the treehouse SHAKES!

"Whoa!" Pinball says. "I didn't know this movie was 3D. Do you have 3D glasses?"

"That's not the movie, you dufus," Night Owl says,

looking around. “Something just shook the Hangout.”

“Um, something like what?” Pinball asks.

“Don’t be ridiculous,” Skunk Girl says, standing up and walking to the edge of the platform. Then, she looks over the edge and says, “You guys are just being—AHHHH!”

“What?” Night Owl asks. “What is it?”

Skunk Girl turns and her face is as white as a ghost.

“What’s going on?” Selfie asks.

“Th-There’s a… a…,” Skunk Girl stammers.

“A what?” Pinball asks. “What is it?”

“A-A monster!” Skunk Girl blurts out. “There’s a monster climbing up the ladder!”

Meta Profile
Next Gen 2.0
Epic Zero
Class: Meta Manipulator
Meta :
Dog-Gone
Class: Meta-Morph
Meta :
Night Owl
Class: Energy Manipulator
Meta :
Skunk Girl
Class: Energy Manipulator
Meta :
Selfie
Class: Magic
Meta :
Pinball
Class: Meta-Morph
Meta :

THREE

I MAKE A BIG MISTAKE

That Skunk Girl has quite the sense of humor.

I mean, just a few seconds ago we were watching a horror movie called Zombie Buffet when we heard strange noises coming from outside. Then, something shook the Hangout pretty hard. And now, after going to investigate, Skunk Girl claims there's a real-life monster climbing up the treehouse ladder.

I'll tell you, that Skunk Girl is a real prankster. I'm not sure how she made those noises and shook the Hangout, but I'm not falling for it. Nope, not this time.

Except, either she's a really good actor or that look of sheer terror on her face is real.

"Didn't you hear me?" Skunk Girl yells. "Run!"

Suddenly, a purple, hairy hand lands on the platform and everyone SCREAMS.

"Quick!" Night Owl yells. "Knock over the ladder!"

"Too late!" Pinball cries, as his popcorn goes flying.

Then, a gigantic figure leaps onto the platform with a THUD, bouncing us off the floor. As I scramble to my feet, I take in the monstrosity before us. Whoever he is, he's absolutely huge—with thick, rounded shoulders and a purple, fur-covered body. He almost looks like a massive gorilla, except when I look into his purple eyes, I notice his vacant expression, like he's not all there.

Yet, for some reason, he looks vaguely familiar. I feel like I should know him, but I can't figure out why. And then I notice a strange, orange glow coming off his body.

What's that about?

But instead of attacking, the monolith stands at the edge of the platform, looking at each of us in turn until his intense gaze lands on me! It's like he's evaluating me.

Then, it hits me where I've seen him before. But… that's impossible. Of course, I didn't recognize him because he's not supposed to be here.

He's supposed to be… dead!

"You okay, Epic Zero?" Night Owl asks.

Not really. But right now, I'm so stunned I can't even find the words to respond. I mean, the last time I saw the villain standing before me, he was vaporized at Lockdown in the battle between Meta-Taker and the Skelton High Commander!

So, how is he here?

"Well, I'll take charge then," Night Owl says, stepping forward. "And I think it's time we returned this grape ape to the zoo."

"W-Wait!" I blurt out. "I mean, don't get too close. I don't know what's going on here, but that's no zoo animal. Th-That's the Berserker. And he was a Meta 3 Strong-man with incredible strength."

"Um, why are you speaking in the past tense?" Selfie asks. "He's standing right here, you know?"

"Because you don't understand," I say. "He died!"

"Died?" Pinball says. "Well, if he's dead then I'm a delicate flower."

I look back at the Berserker, who furrows his brow and bellows, "MMEETTAA PPOOWWEERR!"

Um, what? Meta power?

And then he steps towards me in an abrupt, herky-jerky manner. What's wrong with him? The way he's moving, it's almost like he's a… a… zombie?

"Okay, let's call this a wrap!" Night Owl says, stepping in front of me. Then, she grabs a shadow from the floor and wraps the Berserker from head-to-toe in a shadow-net.

But clearly, it's not going to be that easy because the Berserker flexes and the shadow-net shatters like it was nothing! Then, the Berserker backhands Night Owl who SMASHES into the wall and lands on the floor.

"Night Owl!" I call out, but she doesn't answer.

And when I look back, the Berserker is still lumbering towards me!

"Hey, back off!" I yell.

"I've got it," Skunk Girl says, stepping in front of me to face the Berserker. "Okay, slow poke, get ready to be sick to your stomach!" Then, she unleashes a barrage of stink fumes right in the Berserker's face.

But the Berserker lumbers through it and screeches, "MMEETTAA PPOOWWEERR!"

Even though I'm standing behind her, Skunk Girl's putrid odor reaches my nostrils and I gag, but it's having no effect on the Berserker at all. And then, with shocking speed, he reaches out and grabs Skunk Girl by the wrist. She screams as her body suddenly lights up with the same orange glow that's surrounding the Berserker!

"Skunk Girl!" Pinball yells.

The next thing I know, Skunk Girl's orange glow fades as the Berserker's orange glow intensifies. And when he releases her, she drops to her knees. What just happened? I mean, as far as I'm aware, the only Meta power the Berserker had was Super-Strength.

"M-My powers," Skunk Girl mutters. "I-I can't feel my powers."

"Time to exit!" Pinball says, and then he bounds across the platform, scoops up Skunk Girl, and bounces out of the Hangout.

"MMOORREE MMEETTAA PPOOWWEERR!" the Berserker cries.

More Meta power? Holy cow! I think I know what's going on. Somehow, the Berserker absorbed Skunk Girl's Meta power. But how?

And then I realize something else. I have the most Meta power out of all of us. Is that why he's so focused on me? Am I letting out some kind of a Meta signal he can read? If so, I've got to draw him away from here before someone else gets hurt. But before I can move—

"My turn," Selfie says, stepping in front of me and raising her magic phone. "How about a big smile?"

"Selfie, no!" I call out.

But it's too late! All I can do is turn away as Selfie pushes the button on her phone which emits a bright, hypnotic flash. It takes a few seconds for my vision to come back, but when it does my worst nightmare is realized, because the Berserker is far from hypnotized—and he's holding both of Selfie's arms!

"Aaaah!" Selfie cries. "Epic! Help!"

"MMEETTAA PPOOWWEERR!"

"Selfie!" I yell. "Let her go!"

I've got to act fast before he does to Selfie whatever it was he did to Skunk Girl—or worse! So, I concentrate hard and throw all of my negation power at the Berserker. There, that ought to do the trick. But instead of simply making his Meta powers disappear, to my surprise, the Berserker himself disappears—taking Selfie with him!

Then, I hear CLATTERING at my feet, and when I look down, I see Selfie's phone spinning on the floor.

OMG! She's… gone!

"Selfie?" I call out at the top of my lungs. "Selfie, where are you? Selfie?"

But there's no answer.

I look at my hands in disbelief. What did I just do? I mean, my powers have never done that before. They only duplicate or negate powers, they don't make people disappear.

Suddenly, a wave of nausea comes over me and it feels like I was punched in the gut. If something bad happened to her because of me, I'll never forgive myself.

But what if it wasn't me?

I mean, could the Berserker have teleported? But if he did, how? He didn't have that kind of power before. But then again, he didn't have the ability to wipe out Skunk Girl's powers before either.

I spot Selfie's phone out of the corner of my eye and pick it up when—

"Epic Zero?" comes Night Owl's weak voice from behind me. "I-I blacked out. What happened?"

I wish I knew, but I can only look at her helplessly and say, "I have no idea."

***

All I feel is a crushing sense of guilt.

Needless to say, I barely managed to fly us back to the Waystation 2.0 without having a total breakdown. I barely talked the whole flight because all I could think about was Selfie. We looked everywhere and still couldn't find her. Where did she go? What did I do?

And poor Skunk Girl. We're hoping what happened to her is temporary, but she still hasn't gotten her powers back. Probably for the first time ever, she didn't say much either.

The only good news was finding Mom waiting for us in the Hangar. I don't know if it was mother's intuition or her Psychic powers, but whatever it was, I sure was glad to see her. I didn't even have to say anything. She just put her arm around my shoulder and led us to the Galley where she had some hot cocoa waiting for us.

When the rest of the Freedom Force arrived, I explained everything that happened—including my big mistake. Unfortunately, no one had any ideas about how the Berserker came back to life or what happened to Selfie. So, basically, we're still at square one.

Just then, I feel a warm tongue licking my fingers.

"No, Dog-Gone," I say, pulling my hand away. "No cocoa for you."

Dog-Gone whimpers and slinks away.

Okay, maybe I was a little harsh, but I have a lot on my mind. I can't believe Selfie is gone. I mean, everything felt normal when I used my powers on the Berserker, so why did it produce such a different result? I look at Selfie's phone sitting on the table and crumple inside.

"Well, I checked the Meta Monitor," Dad says,

returning to the Galley after going upstairs. "There weren't any signals from the Berserker at all. Are you sure that's who it was?"

"I'm positive," I say. "And it wasn't just me. We all saw him. He was like a zombie. A Meta zombie."

"That's for sure," Pinball says, sucking down his hot cocoa which leaves a chocolate mustache. "And I'll never forget him. Can I get a refill?"

"Of course," Mom says, pouring him another mugful. Then, she picks up Skunk Girl's mug and gently puts a hand on her shoulder. "Skunk Girl, are you sure you don't want any?"

"No thanks," Skunk Girl says, forcing a smile. "I mean, I still don't know what happened to my powers, but I'd give them up just to have Selfie back again."

"This has been a big shock for you all," Mom says, rubbing Skunk Girl's back, "but you're safe now. And we'll do everything we can to find Selfie."

I hear the optimism in Mom's voice, but what if we can't find Selfie? What if she's gone forever? I take a deep breath and exhale. Ugh, this is the lowest point of my entire life.

"I realize this may not be the best time for this," TechnocRat says, scampering up Skunk Girl's chair, "but the other big mystery is how the Berserker was able to cancel your powers and whether the effect is temporary or permanent. If you're willing, I'd love to run some analysis on you to see if there is any trace of that strange, orange glow you described. It might reveal some important information that will help us get to the bottom of this mystery."

"Yeah, sure," Skunk Girl says. "I'll do whatever it takes, especially if it helps get our friend back."

"Night Owl and I will come too," Pinball says. "We're a team and teams stick together."

"Thanks, Pinball," Skunk Girl says. "You know, sometimes you're alright."

"Wow, are you actually being nice?" Pinball asks, reaching out his hand to help Skunk Girl to her feet.

"Don't get used to it," Skunk Girl says. "You caught me in a weak moment."

"I would never dream of such a thing," Pinball says. "Hey, Epic Zero, do you want to tag along?"

"Um, I'll catch up with you guys in a bit," I say. "I've… got some things to check out first."

I wait until the team exits before turning to my parents and saying, "I feel like this is all my fault." Suddenly, it's like a dam of emotion bursts inside of me and I start bawling uncontrollably.

"Oh, Elliott," Mom says, hugging me tightly. "It's not your fault. I didn't want to pry, but I knew you had something weighing heavily on your mind."

"Y-Yeah," I say, as tears stream down my face. "I-I'm the one who used my powers on the Berserker and he disappeared with Selfie. Of course, it's my fault."

"Well, you don't know that for sure, son," Dad says.

"It could just be a coincidence."

"That was no coincidence," I say, wiping my eyes.

"Listen, little bro," Grace says, "I know you're upset but whether it was your fault or not, sitting around wallowing in self-pity isn't going to get Selfie back. Instead, why don't you put your energy into finding her?"

I look into Grace's blue eyes and realize she's right. I'm not the victim here and crying about it isn't going to solve anything. It's time to stop feeling sorry for myself and go find her.

I leap out of my chair.

"Where are you going?" Mom asks.

"To find Selfie!" I say.

But first I need to change out of these bowling shoes. Dog-Gone trails behind as I stop in my room for my real boots, and then I make my way down the hall and up the twenty-three steps to the Monitor Room.

"Sorry about earlier, bud," I say.

Dog-Gone yips, accepting my apology.

I hop into the command chair and pull up the Berserker's information. It's weird that Dad couldn't find any Meta signals from the Berserker. I mean, we all saw him use some kind of Meta power on Skunk Girl, so it should be traceable.

But when the Meta Monitor finally updates, I'm not looking at the Berserker's Meta Profile, but rather a very large word that's flashing on the screen over and over again. It reads: SHOW.

SHOW?

What's that supposed to mean?

Did TechnocRat update the operating system or something? Then, the word finally fades away and up pops the Berserker's profile. That's him alright—big, hairy, and downright scary. But his status still says DECEASED. So, what's going on here?

Epic Zero!

I jump out of my chair at the sound of my name and look behind me, but no one's there.

That's weird? Who called my name?

Epic Zero, we need your help!

Okay, there it is again. But this time it sounded like it came from inside my head!

That's it. I've officially gone crazy.

Epic Zero, it's Zen! We're being attacked by Meta zombies! Come quickly! Help us! Hurry!

Meta Profile

Airstream

Name: George Mitchell	Height: 5'10"
Race: Human	Weight: 190 lbs
Status: Villain/Active	Eyes/Hair: Brown/Brown

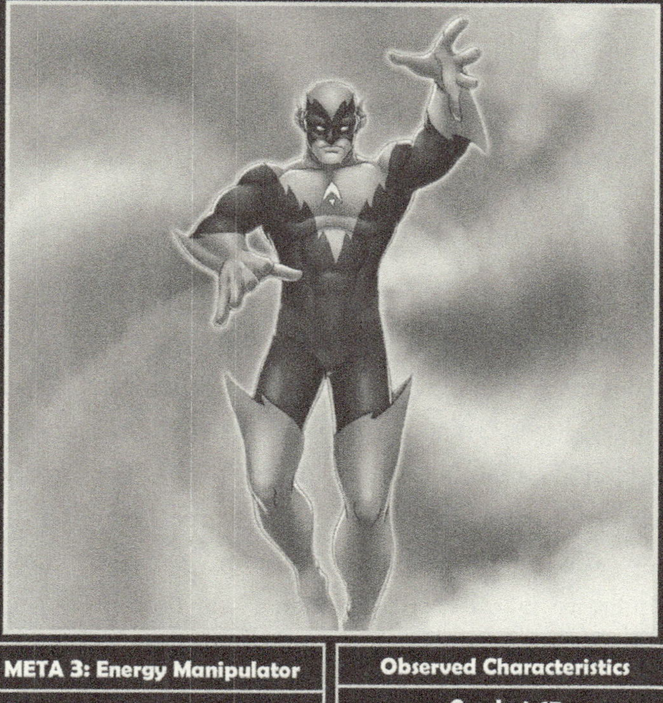

META 3: Energy Manipulator
Extreme Air Current Generation
Can Use Air Currents to Fly

Observed Characteristics			
Combat 67			
Durability	34	Leadership	45
Strategy	76	Willpower	66

FOUR

I GET SWARMED

Japan was the last place I expected to be right now.

But even with everything going on, there was no way I would ignore Zen's mental plea for help. Zen is a good friend and a member of the Rising Suns, the premier superhero team of the East. The last time I saw her, the Rising Suns were the Skelton Emperor's prisoners during his quest to take over the planet. Even though we won that fight, the consequences were awful since Tsunami, her teammate, lost his life in the process.

We can't repeat that again.

Zen's voice sounded desperate when she reached out to me, but her actual message was even more concerning. After all, she said the words 'Meta zombies,' which was just like the Berserker, except plural. He was a handful all by his lonesome, so I can't even imagine what it'll be like to face more than one.

That's why the big guns are going on this mission. Dad, Blue Bolt, Makeshift, and Master Mime are here, while Mom, Grace, Shadow Hawk, and TechnocRat stay behind to keep an eye on things and help Next Gen. And there was no way I was letting Dog-Gone in on this one.

Besides, I had to fight to get on this mission myself. Mom wanted me to rest but I finally convinced her to let me go since I was the one who Zen reached out to. Mom wasn't happy but she had no choice. Of course, who knows what she mentally told Dad.

Anyway, what counts is that I'm here. My primary goal is to help Zen and the Rising Suns, but I'm also hoping to get some answers along the way. Like, what happened to Selfie? It can't be a coincidence that Meta zombies are popping up in both the United States and Japan. The question is why?

Dad guides the Freedom Flyer beneath a bank of clouds and we get our first look at Tokyo below. It's a dense city, packed with buildings of all shapes and sizes. But what really stands out is the Tokyo Skytree, the tallest tower in the world rising over two thousand feet high. Believe me, I wish we were here for sightseeing, but unfortunately, we have far more pressing business on our hands.

"Multiple Meta signals at eight o'clock," Dad says,

reading the dashboard. "Strangely, I only see Meta signatures from the Rising Suns. Get ready team, we should have visuals in twenty seconds."

I lean forward and realize I won't have to wait twenty seconds, because I already see plumes of black smoke billowing up from the city center, along with leveled buildings, overturned cars, and cracked roadways.

But that's not all.

In the middle of the chaos, it looks like there's a small band of ants fending off hundreds of other ants. Except, I know they aren't ants—they must be Meta zombies—and they're closing in on the Rising Suns! I try counting them all but there are just so many of them I can't keep track. If I didn't know better, I'd say there's at least a hundred.

"Prepare for landing," Dad says.

Dad lowers the landing gear, and before I know it, we've touched down behind a demolished parking garage, completely hidden from view. I hear seat belts unclicking behind me and Dad says—

"Listen, this is a simple rescue mission. Our objective is to get the Rising Suns out of here as quickly as possible. If these zombies are anything like Elliott described, they may be able to take away our powers. Don't waste time duking it out with them and don't get yourself cornered. Is that clear?"

"Clear," Blue Bolt and Makeshift say in unison while Master Mime gives a thumbs up.

Then, Dad turns to me and says, "Elliott, when Zen reaches out please let her know we're on our way. But I agreed with your mother that you need to stay here in the Freedom Flyer where it's safe."

"Wait, what?" I say. "I knew she mentally said something to you! That's not fair!"

"Listen, son, you've been through enough recently," Dad says. "Promise me you'll stay here."

I stare into his eyes and I can see he's not going to budge. "Fine," I say, crossing my arms and slumping down in my seat. "I promise."

"Thank you," Dad says, popping the hatch. "Freedom Force—It's Fight Time! Oh, and Elliott, lock up until we get back."

Then, the heroes leap out and they're gone. I close the hatch and press the lock button. Then, I focus my mind, hoping to hear Zen reaching out but there's nothing. I hope she's okay.

Unfortunately, Dad parked behind this wreck of a parking garage so I can't see a thing. I push a few buttons on the dashboard and get five Meta signals on the radar. There's Dad, Blue Bolt, Makeshift, Master Mime… and Zen! Great, she must be okay. But what happened to the rest of the Rising Suns? I don't see anything for the Green Dragon, Fight Master, or Silent Samurai?

Does that mean they're knocked out? Or maybe the Meta zombies stole their powers just like the Berserker did to Skunk Girl? And why don't these Meta zombies show a Meta signal? I mean, I know they're out there. I saw them with my own eyes. This is so weird.

I know I promised Dad I'd stay in the Freedom Flyer, but now I'm worried. I mean, if those Meta zombies got a powerful hero like the Green Dragon, then Dad and the Freedom Force might be in more trouble than they realize. I can't just sit here and let something bad happen to them.

Just as I unclick my seatbelt, a big chunk of rubble slides down the parking garage heap and THUNKS against the hood of the Freedom Flyer, making me jump. Boy, that surprised me. It's so quiet here I guess I'm a little skittish.

But as soon as I stand up, a hunk of cement comes hurtling off the pile and SMACKS against the windshield, startling me. Um, how did that happen? There's no one around but me.

Suddenly, I see something moving in the middle of the rubble. And when I lean forward to see what it is, an object pops through! Except, it's not an object, it's… a hand?

BOOM!

My ears ring and I turn away as debris suddenly rains down on the Freedom Flyer! And when I turn back I see something moving. Coming my way.

It's… a man!

He's broken through, lumbering awkwardly towards me! His skin is pale and he's wearing a ripped red-and-orange costume with a flame insignia on it. And when I stare into his empty, yellow eyes a chill runs down my spine!

It's Flameout—the Meta 3 villain who can turn into pure fire! But… he also died at Lockdown, along with the Berserker! But now he's back!

And he's not alone! Suddenly, more dead Meta villains appear behind him, climbing over the rubble. I see Black Cloud, and Ripcord, and Amphibia! And that's when it dawns on me. They're not here by accident. They're coming for me, just like the Berserker did!

How did they even know I was here?

Well, I can't worry about that now because I've got to scram. Fortunately, I'm in the Freedom Flyer so I should be out of here in no time. I jump into the pilot's chair, flip on the controls, and get ready for lift-off. Except, when I hit the ignition, I don't lift off! In fact, the Freedom Flyer feels like it's being dragged backward!

I call up the rearview camera and get the shock of my life! Dozens of other zombies are holding the Freedom Flyer down! Where did they come from?

"WARNING: THRUSTER JETS CRITICALLY DAMAGED," the Freedom Flyer reports.

What? I look out the window and find Meta zombies tearing my left-wing thruster to pieces. And when I turn right it's the same thing! Then, I'm rocked hard as the zombies start shaking the Freedom Flyer.

SCREEECH! SCREEEEEEEECH!

Holy cow! They're pulling the Freedom Flyer apart to get to me! I'm trapped!

I feel myself hyperventilating but I've got to stay calm. Okay, I need to get out of this ship. I can't take off, but I can… That's it! I snap in my seatbelt, flip open the armrest, and smash the eject button.

FWOOM!

The next thing I know, the hatch pops off and my stomach goes topsy-turvy as I'm catapulted hundreds of feet into the air. I look down and see the blank faces of my adversaries shrinking away, and then I'm long gone.

Unfortunately, so is the Freedom Flyer.

As my momentum slows, I work the touchpad to activate the propulsion jets mounted to the bottom of my chair. Fortunately, they engage, and I steer myself north toward the action and the Freedom Force.

It doesn't take long to find them.

Down below, I see Dad and the others, but they're surrounded by Meta zombies! But that's not all! Dad is the only one moving. And the mindless monsters are pushing up against some kind of invisible force field encircling the heroes.

But how's that possible? Dad can't do that.

And that's when I see Zen. She's standing dead center with her arms outstretched. She must be using her telekinesis to keep those zombies at bay. Now I know why she didn't get back to me.

SPUTTER! PUTT! PUTT!

Uh-oh, I'm going down! I forgot the pilot's chair doesn't hold much fuel. I've got to find somewhere to touch down, but this place is crawling with zombies!

That's when I realize something. When I used my negation powers on the Berserker he disappeared. So, if I use my powers on a lot of these zombies then maybe I can clear my own landing zone. The thing is, I'm gonna have to be precise so I don't make Dad and the other heroes disappear like I did Selfie.

I may be about to make another big mistake, but if I don't try something I'm a goner. So, at around fifty feet, I take a deep breath and hyper-focus my negation power on an area just to the right of the force field. And then, just like that, all of the zombies in that area suddenly disappear!

"Epic Zero?" Dad says, clearly shocked to see me.

"Oh, hey there, Captain Justice," I say, waving weakly as my chair sputters to the ground. "Sorry to drop in like this."

But as soon as I touch down, all of the zombies suddenly turn my way! Then, they come for me!

"Epic Zero!" Dad calls out.

I unclick my seatbelt and stand up, but before I can tell Dad that I'll take care of the rest, he says—

"Zen, open the bubble! We've got to save him!"

"No!" I yell back.

But as soon as I try to move, I can't!

In fact, I can't move a muscle! It's like I'm… frozen?

"Stay there!" Dad calls out. "I'm coming!"

I want to shout 'no,' but I can't even move my mouth. I'm literally locked in place, except for my eyes. I-I don't understand. What's going on?

I see Dad running towards me when all of the Meta zombies suddenly close ranks around him. Dad skids to a stop and tries to jump out of the fray, but the zombies swarm him.

'Dad!' I try calling out, but there's no sound. I dig deep to push out my negation power but nothing happens. The zombies are piling on top of him!

'Someone, help him!' I think, but when I look at the other heroes all I see are more zombies!

"Epic Zero!" Dad yells.

And then he's gone—buried beneath a pile of zombies who are glowing with that bright, orange light!

'Stop!' I try calling out.

I need to help him, but I can't!

Why can't I move? What's happening?

Suddenly, my vision gets blurry.

Dad's cries echo in my ears but I can't see him.

And then everything goes black.

Meta Profile

The Berserker

Name: Unknown	Height: 7'2"
Race: Unknown	Weight: 613 lbs
Status: Villain/Deceased	Eyes/Hair: Purple/Purple

META 3: Super-Strength
Extreme Strength
Extreme Invulnerability
Extreme Agility

Observed Characteristics			
Combat 90			
Durability	95	Leadership	12
Strategy	29	Willpower	84

FIVE

I TAKE A MEETING

"Dad!" I call out.

This time, to my surprise, my voice echoes loud and clear all around me. And that's not all! I can move again! I try opening my eyes but my lashes are stuck together. After a little effort, I manage to pry them open, only to find myself engulfed in complete darkness.

I reach into my utility belt and pull out my flare. But once it's lit, I realize I'm standing inside a narrow, underground tunnel. How on earth did I get down here?

I extend the flare from side to side but all I see is dirt and rock. Where am I? Then, I hear water trickling overhead, which means I'm not just underground but deep underground.

Suddenly, my entire body feels clammy.

I hate being underground!

What am I doing here? This makes no sense.

Just a few seconds ago, I was in the middle of Tokyo helplessly watching Dad get overrun by Meta zombies. And now… well, I've got no clue where I am. But I can't stay here. Dad, Zen, and the others need my help!

Maybe I'm just having a nightmare. Maybe I'll wake up safe and sound next to Dog-Gone slobbering all over my pillow. Boy, it'll be great to see him again—bad breath and all.

But when I reach out and touch the wall it feels too realistic to be a dream. In fact, the rocks are bone-chillingly cold and their edges are super sharp. So, there's no way this is a dream.

Maybe I'll be trapped down here forever!

Right as I'm about to go into full-throttle panic mode, I see something move out of the corner of my eye and gasp. It's a shadow—of a man! I freeze. But just as quickly as it appeared, it's gone!

Okay, am I seeing things? My head tells me to call out to see if he's real, but my gut tells me that's probably not a good idea. So, I stand stock-still and wait for him to come back.

Except, he doesn't. I stay perfectly still for a few minutes but there's no movement and no sounds other than the trickling water overhead and the pounding of my own beating heart.

I don't think he's coming back so I guess the next

move is mine. Either I risk heading his way to see if I'm imagining things, or I play it safe and go the other way. I debate the merits of each option in my mind, and finally conclude that if someone else is down here, he might know the way out.

So, I raise my flare and move forward.

After walking several cautious feet, I reach a bend in the tunnel and peek around, only to hear—

"Please, Elliott Harkness," comes a warm, familiar voice, "join me in my office."

Instantly, the hairs on the back of my neck stand on end. I-I know who it is.

But it can't be. Can it?

I swallow hard and step around the bend into a small, rocky chamber. And sitting in its center, leaning back in his chair with his feet propped up on his desk, is the purple-skinned fiend I hoped I'd never see again.

Tormentus!

"Oh, don't be shy," he says, his yellow eyes narrowing. "Have a seat." Then, he waves his purple hand and a chair magically appears out of nowhere.

Trust me, sitting down with him is the last thing I want to do, but suddenly my legs start moving against my will and don't stop until they plant me firmly in the seat across from him.

"There you go," Tormentus says. "Isn't that more comfortable? Let's put out that flare. We have plenty of light." Then, he waves his hand again and my flare snuffs out as the room gets mysteriously brighter.

That's when it hits me.

"You made me freeze," I say. "You're the one who prevented me from helping Captain Justice and the others."

"Guilty as charged," Tormentus says with an ear-to-ear grin. "But you don't have to call him by his formal name. I know he's your father, remember?"

That's right! I first met Tormentus when I was searching for Beezle. Tormentus told me it was his business to know things, including the secret identities of my parents and me. I thought I was done with him after he took Siphon's soul, but clearly, I was wrong. I don't know what he's up to, but something tells me I'm not going to like the answer.

"What do you want?" I ask firmly.

"Please, relax," Tormentus says. "It's been a while since we've seen one another and I thought it would be good to catch up. Besides, my Meta zombie army has things well under control, so we have plenty of time to get reacquainted."

Suddenly, I feel like I've been hit by a truck.

"*Your* Meta zombie army?" I say, totally shocked. "You mean, you're responsible for all of this? You're the one who brought those villains back from the…"

Then, everything hits me at once.

How could I have been so stupid? Of course, it's Tormentus! After all, Tormentus makes deals in exchange for people's souls. So, he must have made bargains with those dead Metas and is somehow bringing them back to life as zombies! But how? And… why?

"I see the gears turning," Tormentus says, putting his hands behind his head, "but you still look puzzled. Would you like me to explain?"

Drat. I didn't want to give him the edge by seeming clueless but I guess it's written all over my face. "Um, yeah," I say, "if you don't mind."

"It would be my pleasure," Tormentus says. "You see, I realized I didn't properly introduce myself the first time we met. So, let's start with the basics. You may not realize it, but you are sitting with royalty. For I rule over one of the seven kingdoms of the Underworld."

Um, can we rewind that?

Did he just say 'Underworld?'

"My kingdom is known by many names," he continues. "Some call it 'Purgatory,' others call it 'the In Between,' but you can think of my realm as the first stop in your soul's journey between the Overworld—which is your current plane of existence—and its final destination, wherever fate shall determine that to be."

I'm trying to follow him, but if what he's saying is true, then who is this guy? And why does the 'In Between' sound so familiar?

"I hold many titles, including Soul Snatcher of the Underworld and the Supreme Ruler of the In Between. But while my realm is vast and my responsibilities great, I have grown bored of doing the same thing over and over again. Torturing souls and defending my borders simply doesn't hold my interest like it used to. Sure, I could crush my enemies and dominate the seven kingdoms, but why bother? In the end, it is an empty prize."

I nod my head like I'm understanding, but the way he's talking, he's making it sound like he's some kind of a… a… demon lord?

"However, things are different on your plane," he says, flashing a disturbing smile. "After all, humans in the Overworld possess something that's been extinguished by the time they reach my kingdom. Do you know what that is?"

"Um, no," I say. "Not really."

"Free will," Tormentus says. "Humans in the Overworld operate according to free will. Unlike in the Underworld, on your plane I can utilize my superior talents of persuasion and intellect to their full potential. I can literally strike billions of bargains. I can feel… alive!"

His smile sends a chill down my spine.

"Thus, my revelation," Tormentus continues. "Why settle for ruling over a dismal, dead empire when I could rule over an entire realm of living, thinking beings? The choice is obvious. I will rule the Overworld. I will break the free will of every man, woman, and child. The Overworld will be my playground and shaping humanity's future will be my game."

I swallow hard. Is that what this is all about? He

wants to rule the Overworld?

"My army will not fail me," Tormentus says, cracking his knuckles. "But there is one detail in the fine print that may prevent me from completing my plan. And that's where you come in."

Me? I knew he brought me here for a reason.

"And, um, what's that?" I ask, fearing the answer.

Tormentus stares directly into my eyes and says, "Meta energy."

"M-Meta energy?" I repeat.

"That's right," he says, pulling his feet off the desk and sitting up in his chair. "Unfortunately, based on the infernal laws of the Underworld, I'm unable to remain in the Overworld without a constant supply of Meta energy. So, to remain in the Overworld, I need a reliable solution."

Okay, where is he going with this?

"Fortunately, I struck a bargain with a new business partner," Tormentus continues. "With his help, we turned my collection of lost souls into a Meta-draining army capable of stripping Metas of their Meta energy for my personal use. But once that Meta energy has run out there will be nothing left to sustain me, and I will be forced back to the Underworld. However, if I had a constant, uninterrupted supply of Meta energy, well, then I could stay in the Overworld forever."

Suddenly, I get a bad feeling. By the way he's looking at me, he either thinks I'm a juicy steak or the source of this uninterrupted supply of Meta energy! I don't know what he's got planned, but something tells me I don't want to find out!

"Wow," I say, trying to stand up. "That's quite a conundrum you've got there, but I don't think I'm the right guy for the job."

My limbs aren't moving. Why can't I stand up?

"I think I can change your mind about that," Tormentus says. "After all, I have something you want."

Then, he SNAPS his fingers and a masked girl with bright, blue eyes appears beside him.

"Selfie!" I call out.

"Epic!" she cries out as soon as she sees me. She looks scared out of her mind.

Then, Tormentus SNAPS again, and just like that, she's gone.

"Selfie!" I shout. "Bring her back!"

"Are you sure you want her back?" Tormentus asks. "After all, you're the one who sent her to the Underworld in the first place. Truthfully, I wouldn't mind keeping her. I could use the company. It's rare we get a living person in our realm, although it does seem to be happening with greater regularity. Anyway, it's up to you. It does look like she's having a terrible time down there."

"Yes, I'm sure!" I yell. "I'll do anything!"

"That's great news," Tormentus says, "because I have a deal for you. It may seem harsh at first, but I think it's more than fair. Would you like to hear it?"

I nod, bracing myself.

"Perfect," he says. "So, here it is. If you agree to willingly come to the Underworld and do my bidding forever, I'll release your friend back to the land of the living."

"Um, what?" I say, in shock.

"Now, don't answer before you think about it," he says, "because it's literally a once in a lifetime offer."

I'm stunned. I mean, I'd put Selfie's life before mine every time. But if I do, he'll use me to stay on Earth and rule over humanity forever. This is bad.

Really bad.

"So, Elliott Harkness," Tormentus says, "what's it going to be?"

I-I wish I could answer.

But I don't know what to do.

SIX

I GET AN OFFER I CAN'T REFUSE

He's got me and he knows it.

Tormentus just made me an offer I don't think I can refuse. He said he'll return Selfie to the Overworld if I agree to do his bidding in the Underworld—forever! I don't exactly know what his 'bidding' entails, but it sure doesn't sound good. But then again, I don't know of any other way to get Selfie back on my own.

And right now, I'm haunted by how terrified Selfie looked when Tormentus showed her to me. I've never seen her so scared. And it's all my fault.

None of this would have happened if I didn't use my powers on the Berserker zombie. Selfie would be here by my side instead of being held prisoner in Tormentus' Underworld kingdom. And that's the other problem.

It's not like Selfie is in the next town over. I've got no clue how to get to the Underworld to save her, so this might be my only option.

But if I do go with him, he'll use my powers somehow to stay on Earth forever. Then, he'll rule 'the Overworld,' as he calls it—which basically means all of humanity. I'm no odds-maker, but I'd call this a lose-lose situation.

I don't want to sacrifice the planet, but if I don't agree to his bargain Selfie may never get out of the Underworld again. I've got to decide but my brain is so scrambled I can't think straight.

"Well?" Tormentus asks, smiling from ear to ear.

I wish I could slap that grin off his smug, purple face but I still can't stand up. He's holding me down until he gets what he wants. My instincts tell me to reject his offer outright, but maybe that's the wrong decision.

I mean, could I really live with myself if I just skipped out of here without guaranteeing Selfie's safe return? After all, she's, well, kind of special to me. I can't just leave her in the Underworld to rot.

Of course, if I agree to his bargain all of humanity will be doomed. But then again, isn't something bound to doom humanity eventually? I mean, it's only a matter of time before some bad guy destroys the world, right? I stare into Tormentus' eyes and his smile widens.

Okay, I know what I need to do.

I need to right the wrong I caused.

I open my mouth to agree to his terms when—

'STOP!' comes a girl's voice from inside my head.

Huh?

"Whatever you are, get out!" the voice calls out.

Wait a minute. I know that voice.

Just then, it feels like something lifts from my head, like I was wearing a helmet I didn't even know about, and suddenly my mind feels clearer. What happened?

"Epic Zero, can you hear me?" comes the voice again, but this time I know exactly who it is.

"Yes, Zen," I say, touching my fingers to my temples.

"No!" Tormentus yells as he stands up.

Then, everything goes wavy, and Tormentus, the rocky tunnel, the desk, and the chairs disappear! The next thing I know, I'm staring into Zen's eyes.

"Epic Zero, can you see me?" Zen asks, waving a hand in front of my face. "Do you hear me?"

"Y-Yeah," I say, shaking off the cobwebs and squinting in the bright sun. "Where am I?"

"T-Tokyo," Zen says, her voice suddenly sounding strained. "I don't know what happened but you froze. And when I entered your head I sensed a dangerous presence lurking inside your mind."

Lurking inside my mind?

Tormentus! He must have been using his Psychic powers to influence my thinking, just like he did when I first met him. And he almost had me. But then I feel heartbroken, because if I'm here, then Selfie is still—

"Epic Zero, I-I need your help," Zen says, and then I notice she's wincing. "I… nearly let down my guard to help you. W-We've got to get everyone out of here. I-I can't hold them off much longer."

Them? Them who?

Then, as my eyes adjust to the light, my jaw drops because we're surrounded by Meta zombies! There are hundreds of them encircling us, stacked five deep, and pounding against some kind of an invisible wall! And that's when I realize what's happening.

Zen must have absorbed me inside her psychic force field, and she's holding the zombies off single-handedly! But there are so many she's straining to maintain her defense. Just then, my foot brushes against something and when I look down I see Dad!

He's lying on his back and he's not looking so good. His eyes are closed, his costume is shredded, and his breathing is shallow. And the rest of the team are lying all around us, in equally bad shape!

I've got to help Zen! She's down on one knee, giving it all she's got. But if she breaks down we're zombie meat! And it's not like we've got an escape plan. After all, those zombies demolished the Freedom Flyer. So, I guess that leaves us with only one option.

"Get ready to drop the force field," I say.

"Wh-What?" Zen says. "Are you crazy?"

"Probably," I answer, looking at all of the threatening faces surrounding us. "But you'll just have to trust me on this one, okay? So, when I say 'go,' drop the force field."

Zen glances up at me and I dig deep, summoning every iota of negation power in my body. I feel a massive surge through my veins as the Meta energy rushes inside of me. I collect it, bundle it, shape it into a tight ball, but I can feel it pushing back, waiting to explode. I… can't… hold it.

Then, I grit my teeth and yell, "Go!"

Zen relaxes her posture, and suddenly, the first wave of zombies topples over as the force field resisting them dissolves. Then, just as the second and third waves trample over the first, I release my negation power in every direction at once. The energy floods out of my body and washes over the Meta zombies. And then, just like that, they're gone.

"Y-You did it!" Zen says amazed.

I did, but more waves are coming. I want to fight back but I feel dizzy, like I'm out of energy. "N-Need to rest a sec," I say, taking a seat on a giant chunk of rubble. I feel like I'm gonna barf.

"What's that?" Zen says, pointing to the sky.

I squint and see something blurry flying towards us—something big with wings. I try focusing on it, but I can't. And then my eyelids flutter and all I see is black.

***

I wake up to BEEPING, and when I open my eyes

there's a rat with a clipboard standing on my chest. Then, I notice an IV in my left arm.

"Medi-wing?" I ask, rubbing my eyes.

"Yep, your favorite spot," TechnocRat says, scribbling down some notes. "I just finished my examination. Do you want the good news or the bad news?"

"I'll take the good news," I say, stretching my back. Then, I realize my brain is so fuzzy I don't even know what I'm doing here. What was the last thing I did again?

"The good news is your vitals look surprisingly normal," TechnocRat says. "Your blood pressure was low when you first arrived but it's stabilized now." Then, he gestures to the IV and says, "Once we get all of these fluids into your body you'll be good to go."

Well, that is good news. But instead of giving me the bad news, TechnocRat just stands there blinking at me.

"And what about the bad news?" I ask, getting up on my elbows. "Didn't you say there's bad news?"

"Oh, yeah," TechnocRat says, stooping to look up my nostrils. "You've got major bats in the cave. You may want to clear those out before I get the others."

Seriously? I'm gonna kill that rat. I roll my eyes, reach for a tissue, and blow my nose.

"Why don't you hold onto that," TechnocRat says as he scrambles down the bedrail. "I'll grab the rest of the team so we can update you on the zombie situation."

The zombie situation? Suddenly, it all comes racing

back. The Meta zombies! Zen! Dad!

Just then, the door opens and Mom, Skunk Girl, Pinball, Night Owl, and Shadow Hawk walk in. But I don't see Grace, Zen, Dad, or the rest of the team. Where are they?

Just then, Dog-Gone pops up and gives me a big, wet slobber.

"Hey, boy," I say, rubbing his muzzle.

"How do you feel?" Mom asks, gently placing her hand on my arm.

"Still a little woozy," I say. But I honestly don't care about myself right now. "Where's Captain Justice, and Zen, and everyone else? Are they okay? Tell me they're okay."

Mom opens her mouth but hesitates.

"Well?" I ask, my voice rising an octave.

"Glory Girl is helping Zen recover in the Galley," Mom says. "But Captain Justice and the others were impacted by the Meta zombies." Then, she looks down and says, "Like Skunk Girl, they've… lost their powers. There are so many of them we set them up in the Combat Room to get some rest until we can figure out what's going on."

"What?" I say, in total disbelief. "That can't be. There's got to be a way to get their powers back, right, TechnocRat?"

"I'm sorry, kid," TechnocRat says, his whiskers drooping. "I've tried everything I can think of, but this is a mystery even *my* super-intellect can't solve. Plus, while you were off on your mission, I ran a full battery of tests on Skunk Girl, and not only are her powers gone but there's also no trace of Meta energy from the zombie who took them. In fact, none of the Meta zombies seem to generate a Meta signature. And just like Skunk Girl, Captain Justice and the others are now, well, Zeroes."

Zeroes?

Just hearing the word makes me feel like I was punched in the gut. I mean, Dad—a Zero? I can't believe it. Suddenly, my mind flashes back to Tokyo and Dad being overwhelmed by Meta zombies. I wanted to help, but there was nothing I could do about it. And it's all because of—

"Tormentus!" I blurt out.

"Tormentus?" Shadow Hawk repeats with a quizzical look on his face. "Isn't that the villain from Safari Park? The one who took Siphon's soul? What does he have to do with this?"

"He's the one responsible for this," I say. "He told me he's tired of being the Soul Snatcher of the Underworld. He said he's declared war against the Overworld, and his army of Meta zombies are going to drain the power of every Meta on the planet."

"Um, did you just say Underworld?" Pinball asks, pointing down. "As in, *that* Underworld?"

"It doesn't matter where he's from," Skunk Girl says. "When I get a hold of him I'll show him who's boss."

"I think getting a hold of him is the problem," Shadow Hawk says. "This character seems pretty shifty. Did you say he called himself the Soul Snatcher?"

"Yeah," I say. "Why?"

"Because I never put two and two together until now," Shadow Hawk says, scratching his chin. "The Soul Snatcher was the reason we formed the Protectors of the Planet in the first place. We banded together to stop him. So, if Tormentus and the Soul Snatcher are the same person, then he's been toying with humans for decades."

"Wait a minute," Night Owl says. "If you faced him before then how did you beat him?"

"We didn't," Shadow Hawk says. "His powers were too immense, even for us. He was on the verge of victory when he suddenly vanished. I still remember the surprised look on his face when it happened. It didn't seem like it was part of his plan and we never saw him again after that."

"Interesting," TechnocRat says, twitching his nose. "I wonder if he was summoned back to the Underworld."

"No," I say, remembering my conversation with Tormentus. "He said he needs Meta energy to stay on our plane. Maybe he ran out?"

"Well, that's even more interesting then," TechnocRat says, "because it can't be a coincidence that he's using his Meta zombies to steal Meta energy. He must be storing it somewhere for his personal use—to keep him here in the 'Overworld,' as you said he calls it.

But where is he storing it? You'd think the Meta Monitor would detect such a large quantity of Meta energy."

"Unless it's not on Earth," Shadow Hawk suggests. "Maybe he's storing it in the Underworld."

BREEP! BREEP! BREEP!

"What's that?" Skunk Girl asks.

"I know that frequency," Mom says, her eyebrows rising. "That's a direct call coming in from Lockdown. To the Mission Room!"

"Hey!" I yell as they all exit the room. "What about… me?"

But they're long gone and I'm stuck here attached to this IV. Fortunately, it's on wheels, so I throw my legs over the bed and roll the IV unit along as I head to the Mission Room. I don't know why Lockdown is calling, but I'm betting it isn't good. Unfortunately, I can't hear the information firsthand, because by the time I reach the Mission Room, Mom is finishing the call.

"We'll send a team right away!" Mom says, and then hangs up as the monitor switches to static. Then, she turns and sees me standing in the doorway. "Epic Zero, what are you doing out of the Medi-wing?"

"Helping," I say. Then, I nod at the IV unit and say, "despite my obstacles. What's the story?"

"That was Lockdown," Mom says. "They've spotted a battalion of Meta zombies approaching in the distance."

"Meta zombies at Lockdown?" I say.

Then, a lightbulb goes off. Of course, Tormentus

would go after Lockdown. After all, where else could he find such a large supply of Meta energy all in one place?

"We've got to stop them!" I say. "Those Meta prisoners are sitting ducks!"

"Yes," Mom says. "But there's no 'we,' here. You need to get back to the Medi-wing to rest while—"

"I'm sorry, but there's no time for rest," I say.

"Excuse me?" Mom says, crossing her arms.

"I appreciate your concern," I say, "but let's face it, I'm the only one here capable of sending those monsters back to where they came from. So, if someone can unhook me from this contraption we can get going already."

Meta Profile
The Rising Suns
Green Dragon
Class: Super Strength
Meta :
Zen
Class: Psychic
Meta :
Fight Master
Class: Meta-Morph
Meta :
Silent Samurai
Class: Magic
Meta :

SEVEN

I FACE AN ONSLAUGHT

Why do all roads lead back to Lockdown?

I mean, I was here only a few weeks ago trying to stop an insane Meta-Man from busting the place wide open. Of course, that didn't go so well, which was how Meta creeps like Airstream and Pulverizer got free in the first place. And speaking of Airstream and Pulverizer, it feels like Dad and I hauled them in a million years ago instead of just yesterday.

So much has changed since then.

Thinking about Dad crushes me. I wish I could have seen him before we left but there just wasn't time. I know things could have been different if Tormentus didn't freeze me. But unfortunately, that's not what happened.

I look out the window as Grace pilots our Freedom

Flyer through the clouds. We'll be at Lockdown soon enough, and if we don't stop those zombies before they reach the prisoners then Tormentus will get his grubby little hands on a huge amount of Meta energy.

Unfortunately, we'll be fighting short-handed. With most of the team out of action, it's basically up to Grace, Pinball, Night Owl, Shadow Hawk, TechnocRat, and me. Honestly, I didn't even want to bring Pinball and Night Owl but Shadow Hawk thought they could be useful. I wish Mom was here, but we all agreed it was better to have her on the Waystation in case things went sideways.

I just hope we can complete this mission quickly. TechnocRat said he has a big plan to keep Lockdown out of reach. I asked him what he meant by that, but he said it's a surprise. Believe me, I trust TechnocRat, but sometimes his 'surprises' worry me. You know, like that time I was almost eaten by a T-Rex while he fiddled with his Time Warper device.

"Look alive, people," Grace says, flicking some buttons on the dashboard. "Lockdown at five o'clock."

I feel a knot in the pit in my stomach as the prison comes into view—and it's far from a sight for sore eyes. I have to say, Dad and TechnocRat did a great job on the repairs because it looks like new. But based on what I'm seeing it's not gonna last long.

Not by a longshot.

"Um, are all of those dots down there what I think they are?" Pinball asks, swallowing hard. "Because if they're zombies, then it kind of looks like there's thousands of them."

He's right about that. There are more Meta zombies lumbering toward Lockdown than were swarming us in Tokyo. The prison guards are doing their best to hold them off but their weapons are useless. The zombies just keep on coming.

I hope I can pull this off, because if I can't…

"I know this might sound weird," Grace says, "but are we thinking about this the right way? I mean, maybe we should just save the guards and let the zombies go to town on the prisoners. After all, if they take away the prisoners' Meta energy aren't they doing us a big favor? There'd be, like, no more bad guys."

"It might seem that way," TechnocRat says, "but if all of that Meta energy is transferred to Tormentus, I fear we'll have an even bigger problem on our hands." Then, he looks out the window and says, "Land near the front entrance. I need to get inside the control room to execute my plan. Everyone should be prepared to take off as soon as you get my signal."

"Roger that," Grace says, adjusting our flight path to land inside the compound.

"How do you feel, kid?" Shadow Hawk asks, patting my shoulder from the seat behind me.

"Good to go," I say, lying through my teeth.

Truthfully, I feel lousy but now isn't the time to shake the team's confidence. They're depending on me.

"Great," Shadow Hawk says. Then, he turns to the others and says, "Remember what we're facing here. This isn't the time for unnecessary heroics. Is that clear?"

"Oh, you won't have to worry about that with me," Pinball says.

"Perfect," Shadow Hawk says. "But just in case, I'd like you and Night Owl to accompany TechnocRat inside Lockdown. If those zombies get past our defenses, he'll need all the help he can get. Glory Girl and I will run interference for Epic Zero while he disposes of the enemy."

Well, he made that sound easy. Not.

I have to say, it's great having Shadow Hawk and his strategic brain with us this time. Besides, he's already a Zero, so he can fight those zombies without worrying about losing his powers.

Of course, if I screw up he could lose more than that—like his life! No pressure.

"Prepare for landing," Grace says.

I clutch my armrests as we touch down smoothly next to the front door. Then, we unhook our seatbelts and Grace pops the hatch. Ready or not, here we go.

"Let's rock, kiddos," TechnocRat says to Pinball and Night Owl as he turns on his jet pack and flies out of the vehicle. "And try to keep up!"

"You've got this," Night Owl says to me before exiting via a shadow slide.

"Don't do anything I wouldn't do," Pinball adds.

"Um, dude, I've got to do something," I say.

"Right, scratch that," Pinball says. Then, he bounces out of the Freedom Flyer.

"You've got some weird friends," Grace says.

"Tell me about it," I say.

"Are you ready?" Shadow Hawk asks.

Grace and I look at each other and nod.

"Alright then," he says with a wink. "Freedom Force—it's Fight Time!"

Grace takes off into the air as Shadow Hawk and I leap out of the Freedom Flyer. It was nice to hear Shadow Hawk use Dad's battle cry, but at the same time, it makes me sad. I wish Dad was here to say it himself, but I'll do my best to make him proud.

Unfortunately, that's gonna take more than I thought, because as soon as we run through the front gates I gasp. Zombies are everywhere—marching our way like an unstoppable, undead army, stretching as far as my eyes can see. And as I assess the monumental task before me, Shadow Hawk's words about Tormentus echo in my brain: *he's been toying with humans for decades.* Well, that must be true, because it must have taken years to bargain with all of these souls!

Suddenly, panic sets in. There are so many of them. I-I'm not sure I can do this.

"Steel yourself, kid," Shadow Hawk says as he pulls out his Hawk-a-rang. "Because we've got less than a minute before they're on top of us."

"Yeah, I've got this," I say, unconvincingly.

"Shouldn't you get started already?" Grace calls out, flying overhead. "There's no time like the present."

"Glory Girl, stay as high as you can," Shadow Hawk says. "Everything should be fine, but if we're about to be overrun, forget about me and get Epic Zero out of here. Got it?"

"Yep," she says, climbing higher, "but let's not let it get to that point. So, you better get cracking."

"Okay, okay!" I say, closing my eyes I've got to focus. I've got to start negating their Meta energy.

GGGGRRRRRRRR!

The proximity of the sound surprises me and I open my eyes to find a gray Meta zombie only four feet away—and he's coming right at me! He's wearing a ripped black and gray costume with the insignia of a cloud on his chest.

Is that Black Cloud?

"Wake up, kid!" Shadow Hawk says, as his Hawk-a-Rang CLANGS against the zombie's skull before circling expertly back into his hand. "It's go time!"

He's right. It's now or never.

I concentrate and pull as much negation power as I can muster, but I can tell it already feels like less than what I had in Tokyo. What gives? I mean, I've never felt a limit to my powers like this.

"Epic Zero?" Shadow Hawk says, knocking Black Cloud back with a kick to the gut.

I take in the massive number of villains before us and feel nervous. But what did Shadow Hawk say? Steel myself? Well, here goes nothing.

I spread my arms and unleash my negation energy, pushing it as far and wide as I can. Suddenly, Black Cloud and hundreds of other zombies disappear at once.

"That's it!" Shadow Hawk says.

Thank goodness. But that only took care of the first wave. There's more coming—lots more.

The problem is, I'm not sure I have anything left in the tank. I probably should have let more of those fluids get into my body before I came down here, but it's too late now.

"Get ready," Shadow Hawk says.

I look in the distance at the next wave coming, and the waves after that. The funny thing is, they seem to be reorganizing themselves, spreading out into a wider circle around us. That's weird. Why are they doing that?

"Guys, look out!" Grace yells. She's pointing at something close. "Look down! Right in front of you!"

Right in front of us? What's she talking about?

But then I look down and do a double take, because coming out of the ground, in the same area where I just negated the zombies, are even more zombies! They're coming back—resurfacing out of the ground!

But how can that be?

"Epic Zero!" Shadow Hawk calls out. "Use your powers!"

Holy smokes! I reach inside to pull up what I can, but I'm just so exhausted it feels like there's nothing left. The next thing I know, Black Cloud emerges again and cuts me off from Shadow Hawk. And now I'm completely surrounded!

RUUUUMMMMBBBBLLLEEE!!!

Suddenly, the ground shakes beneath my feet, and I hear an ear-splitting SCREECH. Just then, a giant shadow blankets us as if something huge is hovering overhead. And when I look up my eyes go wide because Lockdown is rising into the air! But how? And that's when I see eight massive rocket jets firing beneath Lockdown, lifting the entire structure skyward!

For a second, I'm confused, and then I realize this must have been TechnocRat's plan all along! When he said he'd keep Lockdown out of reach, I never would have guessed he meant *this*!

"Surprise!" TechnocRat yells from a window.

Man, that rat is annoying, but I've got to hand it to him, he's a genius.

OOOOOOORRRRRRGGGGG!

I feel hot breath on the back of my neck, and when I spin around, I find a Meta zombie right behind me! I stare into her vacant, yellow eyes and recognize her costume. It's Death Nell! She was a Meta 3 Energy Manipulator who died a long time ago!

I-I want to fight back, but I'm so tired I can't do anything. Is this how it's going to end?

Death Nell reaches for me when I feel someone grab me beneath my armpits and lift me into the air!

"Time to get out of here," Grace says.

"But what about Shadow Hawk?" I ask, looking down. "I don't see him anywhere."

"Don't worry," she says. "He's coming."

FWOOP!

Just then, I see a grappling hook hurtling through the air. The metal claw wraps itself around one of Lockdown's jets and pulls the cable taut. Then, it retracts, pulling Shadow Hawk out from beneath a pile of zombies.

I can't believe it! He made it!

And as we climb into the sky, I'm relieved we accomplished our mission, but terrified by Tormentus' awesome power.

Meta Profile

Black Cloud

▯ Name: Boris Dutreich	▯ Height: 6'0"
▯ Race: Human	▯ Weight: 200 lbs
▯ Status: Villain/Deceased	▯ Eyes/Hair: Blue/Blonde

META 3: Meta-morph
▯ Extreme Gas Manipulation
▯ Can Disperse Body into Toxic Gas Molecules

Observed Characteristics			
Combat 84			
Durability	90	Leadership	62
Strategy	83	Willpower	88

EIGHT

I PUT A RING ON IT

We almost didn't get out of there alive.

Thankfully, we're safe and sound back on the Waystation, but, for a few seconds there, I thought I was a goner. Those Meta zombies were a heartbeat away from capturing me, and then, well, I don't want to think about what might have happened next. Fortunately, Grace rescued me just in time. I definitely owe her one, and I'm sure she won't let me forget it.

As for Lockdown, I had no idea TechnocRat built the facility with massive, emergency rocket jets in case something catastrophic happened. He certainly didn't tell me, and apparently, he failed to mention this enormous detail to anyone else. The way that rat thinks continues to amaze and confound me.

I look through the Galley porthole at the Meta prison orbiting peacefully next to us. TechnocRat is over there now, helping the guards adjust to their new environment while ensuring the facility holds up to the extreme atmospheric pressures of space. Boy, I hope everything is okay because the last thing anyone needs is for that thing to implode on us.

I can't take any more problems right now.

"So, what else do you guys have to eat?" Pinball asks, rummaging through the pantry.

Pinball was starving when we got back, so I brought the gang into the Galley for a snack. Of course, I feel sick to my stomach and can't eat a thing.

"I don't know," I say, absent-mindedly spinning Selfie's phone on the table. "What you see is what we've got."

"Ooooh!" Pinball exclaims as he pulls out the box of Frosted Letter-Bites. "I love these but my parents won't let me have them. Is it okay if I have a bowl?"

"Knock yourself out," I say, realizing there's no one here to object. "Spoons are in the drawer, bowls are in that upper cabinet, and milk is in the fridge."

"Thanks," he says, pouring the dry cereal into a bowl and putting it on the table while he goes for the milk.

"So, what do we do now?" Night Owl asks.

I wish I knew, but I don't have a clue. Tormentus is way more powerful than I imagined, Dad and most of the heroes are powerless, and Selfie is still trapped in the

Underworld. I don't think I've ever felt so hopeless.

CRUNCH! CRUNCH!

"Hey! Stop that!" Pinball yells, and when I look over Dog-Gone's snout is buried deep in Pinball's cereal bowl.

"Eat your own food!" Pinball says, pulling the bowl away as Dog-Gone licks his lips and turns invisible.

I guess no matter how dire the circumstances, nothing can stop the furry mercenary from striking.

I spin Selfie's phone again. I wish she was here right now. I bet she'd know what to do.

Then, I notice something. Her screen looks different. Instead of all the apps, there's just a big, single word flashing on her display screen. It reads: WEAKNESS.

Huh? That's weird.

"Listen, boss-man," Skunk Girl says, "I know you're feeling guilty about Selfie and all, but now is not the time to fold like a chair. She needs our help. Well, given the current state of my powers, I guess she needs *your* help. And you're not going to help her by sulking in this booth. We need some fresh thinking here."

I look into Skunk Girl's eyes and realize she's right. I'm not going to save Selfie if I'm down on myself like this. We need fresh thinking. Fresh thinking and action.

The problem is, I don't even know where to start.

But then again, I know someone who might.

"Where are you going?" Skunk Girl asks.

"I'll be right back," I say, grabbing Selfie's phone and standing up. "You guys finish your snack. C'mon, Dog-

Gone, let them eat in peace."

I leave the Galley and Dog-Gone appears beside me.

"Follow me," I say, taking the stairway down to the Combat Room. I wanted to do this earlier but I couldn't. So, now is my chance to see Dad and get his advice on things. After all, he's led the Freedom Force through more challenging missions than I can count. He'll know what we should do next.

But when we reach the Combat Room my stomach sinks, because the large, white room has been converted into a temporary hospital ward. Beds and medical equipment are organized into neat rows, and the beds are occupied by once-great heroes like Blue Bolt, Master Mime, the Green Dragon, and… Dad.

I see him lying at the end with his eyes closed. He's still in his ripped costume, but he's wearing an oxygen mask and hooked up to various monitoring devices. I want to go over but hesitate.

"Hey," comes a familiar voice from behind.

I turn to see Mom who flashes a weak smile.

"Hey," I say. "I'll… come back later."

"Don't be scared," Mom says. "He's just resting. Go over and sit with him. He'll know you're there and it will mean a lot to him. I'll keep Dog-Gone here with me."

"O-Okay," I say nervously and start walking slowly towards Dad. As I pass the other beds only Blue Bolt is awake and she winks at me. I wave back awkwardly and smile, but I feel so bad for her, so bad for all of them.

When I reach Dad, I hear a low BEEPING noise from the monitor. He's breathing much better than the last time I saw him but it hurts to see him like this. I mean, he was the strongest hero I knew.

And now…

I sit on the edge of the bed.

"H-Hey, Dad," I say, as a tear rolls down my cheek. "I-I just wanted to let you know how sorry I am for what happened. I-I wish I could have helped you. I wish I could have stopped Tormentus from freezing me. I-I wish… I wasn't so weak."

I tap Selfie's phone against my palm and out of the corner of my eye I see that word again. WEAKNESS.

Then, it dawns on me that I've seen a lot of random words lately. There was that one flashing on the Meta Monitor. SHOW. Then, there was that one in my bowl of cereal. What was that one again? NEVER?

WEAKNESS. SHOW. NEVER.

Why does that seem so—

Suddenly, a shockwave runs through my body.

WEAKNESS. SHOW. NEVER.

NEVER. SHOW. WEAKNESS.

OMG! I-I know those words. But that can't be a coincidence, can it? And then two things hit me at once.

One, the last time I saw K'ami, she said she was in a place called 'the In Between.' And two, that's the same name Tormentus used for his kingdom!

So, why am I seeing these words—K'ami's words—

now? Is it just a coincidence, or is she sending me a message from beyond?

And then I realize something else. Selfie is Tormentus' prisoner in the Underworld. Could K'ami be with Selfie?

I jump off Dad's bed and start pacing. I mean, this is just too specific to be a coincidence. K'ami must be reaching out to me. She must be trying to tell me something—but what? Then, a lightbulb goes off.

Suddenly, I know exactly what I need to do.

I need to go to the Underworld.

Yes, it sounds nuts, but if I'm gonna stop Tormentus and save Selfie, I'm not going do it up here in 'the Overworld,' as Tormentus calls it. I'm going to have to do it down there—where he may be storing his Meta energy. It's a gamble, but it's a risk I've got to take.

But how will I get there? I mean, as far as I know, there aren't any flights heading to the Underworld. And I definitely don't want to go there the traditional way, if you know what I mean.

"Are you okay?" Mom asks, nearly making me jump out of my skin. "I don't want to pry but it looks like you have a lot on your mind."

"Oh, yeah," I say, stopping my pacing. "I'm good."

"Is there anything I can do to help?" Mom asks.

I wish I could tell Mom what's going on, but if I do she'll never let me go. I wish I could tell her. I wish…

Wait a minute? Wish? That's it!

"Elliott?" Mom asks. "Do you need anything?"

"Um, no," I say, trying to stay calm so she'll think everything is okay and will stay out of my thoughts. "Now that I've visited Dad, I-I think I'll go back upstairs to hang out with my friends."

"Okay," she says with a suspicious look on her face. "I know this is hard. Remember, I'm always here if you need me."

"Thanks," I say, hugging her. "C'mon Dog-Gone." I exit the Combat Room calmly and then, as soon as I'm out of sight, I book up the stairs as fast as possible. I hate not being truthful with Mom, but I have no intention of seeing my friends.

I've got other plans.

I exit the stairwell, but instead of turning toward the Galley, I head the other way.

WOOF!

Uh-oh. I forgot about Dog-Gone. His body is pointed toward the Galley but he's looking back at me.

"You go ahead," I say. "I'll, um, be there soon."

But Dog-Gone doesn't move and I get the sense he knows I'm not telling him everything.

"Go on," I say. "Tell you what, you can eat all the cereal you can get your muzzle on until I get back. Deal?"

Dog-Gone's tail wags and he takes off, turning invisible right before he enters the Galley. I feel bad doing that to Pinball, but I've got to get moving.

I race through the halls until I reach my destination—

the Trophy Room. The Trophy Room is an area that's filled with display cases holding all sorts of strange and assorted souvenirs from the Freedom Force's various missions. Some of the items are simply fun, like Mr. Mint's giant quarter or the Mad Popper's Bubble Gum Gun, while others are more, well, dangerous.

I ignore everything else and make a beeline for a display case sitting in the corner. The plaque on the stand reads: *The Three Rings of Suffering. Extremely Dangerous. Do not remove from glass. DO NOT WEAR UNDER ANY CIRCUMSTANCES.*

I take a deep breath.

And then I remove the glass cover.

I stare at the two rings sitting innocently on the stand. One is bronze and the other is silver, but both have lightning bolt symbols carved into their faces. Just looking at them sends a shiver down my spine.

After all, each Ring of Suffering contains one of the Djinn Three, evil genie brothers who have plagued mankind for centuries. Beezle won't be useful since I trapped him in his silver ring for all of eternity. And I have no clue where Terrog and his gold ring are. So, that leaves me with one ticket to the Underworld.

Rasp.

I pick up his bronze ring and exhale.

I mean, am I really going to do this?

But then I think of Selfie and K'ami and slip the ring on my finger.

NINE

I GO DOWN UNDER

I shield my face as the bronze ring sparks with electricity.

And then, the next thing I know, out swirls a gray, spirit-like creature who swells up to ten feet tall. He's just as ugly as Beezle, and by the look of sheer disgust on his face, I can tell there's no need for introductions.

"Um, hey there, Rasp," I offer.

"YOU!" Rasp practically spits. "*You* dared to summon *me*?"

Suddenly, it dawns on me that this was probably a huge mistake. After all, when I was Beezle's master I used my last wish to trap him inside his own ring for all of eternity. And right before he obeyed my command, Beezle told me his brothers would avenge him.

So, like the genius I am, I've now given Rasp his

opportunity to get me back.

Just. Freaking. Wonderful.

"Yes, I summoned you," I say as confidently as I can. "I need your help."

"Well, I refuse," Rasp says, crossing his arms and turning his back on me. "I refuse to help the sworn enemy of my brother. So, I suggest you simply remove the ring and I will return to my home."

"Um, that's not how this works," I say, holding out my ring finger. "I'm wearing the bronze ring, see? Which means I'm your master now and you know it."

Rasp scrunches his gray face in anger, and if he could turn red I'm pretty sure he'd look like a flaming tomato right now.

"Indeed," he says after a long pause, looking at me from over his shoulder. "That is correct. As you are now the bearer of the bronze Ring of Suffering, you are my master and I am at your service. But I do not have to like it."

"Works for me," I say with a shrug.

"As you undoubtedly know by now," Rasp says matter-of-factly, "I am here to fulfill your utmost desires. I can grant you three wishes. However, there are limitations. I am not able to bring the dead back to life and I am not permitted to grant you unlimited wishes. You have three wishes at your disposal. So, let's get this over with if we must. Now tell me, what do you desire… master?"

Well, it definitely took him a lot of effort to get that last word out. Believe me, I'm not thrilled about partnering with an evil genie with attitude problems either, but I need him to get me to the Underworld and back again.

Unfortunately, traveling to the Underworld is going to use two of my three available wishes. I mean, I don't know what I'm going to run into when I actually get down there, but I'm pretty sure it's not going to be rainbows and unicorns. Frankly, this whole situation terrifies me, but this is my only shot so I've got to take it.

But that's not my only concern.

Based on my experience with Beezle, I need to make sure my wishes are as specific as possible. Beezle tricked me by intentionally twisting my words and I can't let that happen again. I'll also need to keep close tabs on my mental state. Especially since each Djinn can warp minds, and while Rasp is less powerful than Beezle he could still try to influence my thinking.

"Rasp," I say, "I'd like to make my first wish."

"Oooh, how exciting, tiny master," Rasp says dryly.

I roll my eyes, but before I share my wish I realize I need to think this through. I need to get into the Underworld, but where exactly should I go? According to Tormentus, there are seven kingdoms down there so the Underworld must be huge. I guess I could ask Rasp to drop me in Tormentus' kingdom, but I'm sure he'd happily dump me in the middle of some hot mess.

That just seems too risky.

I could ask him to take me to K'ami. I'd love to see her again, but what if I read those clues wrong? Even though that message seemed to come from her, I can't be sure. So, the only thing I know for certain is that Selfie is down there and saving her is my number one priority.

"Rasp," I say, "here's my first wish and I want you to listen closely. I want you to take me into the Underworld and make sure I appear right next to Selfie. Is that clear?"

"Your wish left no room for misinterpretation, my insignificant master," Rasp says. "However, if you do wish to travel to the Underworld, I must remind you that I am unable to bring the dead back to life. So, if that is the purpose of this journey, then I am afraid I will not be of service."

K'ami's face flashes through my mind. The last time I saw her she told me she was dead, so there's no chance of me bringing her back.

"That's not why I'm going," I say. "But thank you."

"Very well, my cowardly master," Rasp says. "Now hold on to your cape, because your wish…" Then, he waves his hand, "… is fulfilled."

Suddenly, I'm no longer standing in the Trophy Room, but on a sooty, black surface in a very strange place. Everywhere I look are twisted pathways, some going straight up and others going diagonal or straight down. It's like the laws of gravity don't exist! And the sky above—if you can even call it that—is a mass of dreary, brownish-yellow clouds. Suddenly, my whole body feels really warm and I pull on my neck collar to get some relief.

Is-Is this it? Am I really in the Underworld?

But where is Selfie?

I look up at Rasp who is scratching his chin with a puzzled expression on his face.

"Hey!" I call out. "I told you to make me appear next to Selfie. Where is she?"

"I was just wondering the same thing myself," Rasp says. "I feel like I was properly attuned to her location, but it does seem like there is no one here but us, doesn't it?"

"Don't play dumb with me," I say. "I know you did this on purpose. You're trying to get revenge on me for what I did to your brother. But I'm your master now so you've got to obey me."

"Yes, of course, my shallow master," Rasp says. "But please, believe me, I did not try to sabotage you. At least, not yet. While your friend is not here, I do believe she passed through here recently. It just may be that there are different rules at play when one uses Magic in the Underworld. After all, I can already sense this place has some unusual characteristics, which you no doubt see with your very own eyes. Thus, the use of Magic here may be… unpredictable, to say the least."

Great. I look into Rasp's eyes but I don't know if I can trust what he's saying or not. He has it in for me for sure, but it's also clear this is a very strange place.

"If you would allow me a suggestion, oh lowly master," Rasp adds. "If you would like, you could use another wish and we could simply try again? Perhaps my Magic will be far more accurate since we are now in the Underworld itself. I am certain I could find your friend if you give me a second chance."

I look at Rasp suspiciously. He's trying to bait me into burning my second wish. If I did that, it would leave me with only one wish left and that doesn't seem like a good idea. Especially since I don't know what I'm going to find. And I need to hang on to my final wish to get Selfie and me out of here.

"You know, I'm gonna pass on that," I say. "You said she was here recently so maybe I'll do a little looking around first."

"As you wish, my unconfident master," Rasp says.

"And can you please stop with the insults?" I ask.

"Of course, my less-than-adequate master," he says.

I roll my eyes. Well, this is going to be fun. Now the big question is, where am I supposed to look? All I see are these crazy pathways going in all directions. Some end abruptly while others disappear in the distance.

"Do you know which path she took?" I ask.

"Well, I am a Djinn and not a detective," Rasp says, looking down by my feet. "But if I were you, I might consider following those footprints."

Footprints?

I look down, and to my surprise, there's a set of footprints in the sooty material. I kneel to investigate and realize they're boot prints, about the same size as Selfie's feet! Could they be her footprints?

"Let's go," I say.

I follow the footprints until the pathway suddenly goes straight up at a ninety-degree angle. Yet, somehow, the footprints continue. But how can that be?

I lift my right foot and plant it on the vertical surface. Then, I step up, and to my surprise, the surface holds my weight! I lift my other foot and realize I'm now standing parallel to the pathway I was just on. Okay, this is pretty wild, but I'll have to debate the physics at play here later. Right now, I need to keep following these footsteps.

As I walk straight up, I realize everything feels completely normal, like gravity has adjusted to me instead of me adjusting to it. After I've gone a hundred yards or so the pathway levels off again and widens considerably, connecting to a much larger landmass. But unlike the pathway, the terrain here is much more diverse, with rocky hills, tall stalagmites, and towering mountains.

I continue into a dirt ravine when the footprints suddenly stop. That's strange. It's like the person who made them vanished into thin air.

"What happened?" I ask.

"It appears you have reached the end of the trail, my not-so-observant master," Rasp says. "I do hope your friend did not meet a tragic end."

I'm about to tell him to shut his trap when I notice a towering rock castle in the distance. And then I hear—

"Stop lollygagging and keep moving!"

Someone is coming!

I look for the closest hiding spot and dive behind a rock pillar.

"Get back into your ring," I whisper firmly to Rasp, whose body is floating in plain sight. "They'll see you!"

"Is that a wish?" Rasp asks, raising an eyebrow.

"No, it's an order," I snap. "Now do it!"

"Very well," Rasp says, as he shrinks back into the bronze ring.

I peer around the corner and see a group of people heading our way. But as they get closer, I realize their bodies are transparent like ghosts, and they aren't walking but floating along the surface. Holy cow! Are those… souls?

And that's not all. Behind them, shepherding them along with pronged spears, are two gargantuan figures that set off my alarm bells. They have muscular, human-like bodies, but the heads of bulls! If I didn't know better, I'd say they looked like… Minotaurs? And unlike the ghost people, the Minotaurs look completely solid.

"Keep it moving," a Minotaur says. "We don't have all day to process you sorry bunch."

Process? Hmmm. Isn't that what Tormentus told me. Didn't he say his kingdom was the first stop for souls on their journey?

As they pass by, one of the Minotaurs suddenly turns his head in my direction and I duck out of sight. I hold my breath and stay perfectly still. Hopefully, he didn't see me. As their voices fade away, I wait a long time before braving another look. And when I do I'm relieved to see they're gone.

Whew! That was close.

I wipe the sweat off my brow and step back into the open when I'm suddenly lifted into the air by my cape!

"Well, what do we have here?" comes a deep voice.

I'm shocked as my body swivels around and I suddenly find myself staring into the hair-filled nostrils of a Minotaur! H-How did he get there? I mean, I didn't even hear him.

"You nearly avoided me," he says, as his hot breath hits me square in the face. "I probably wouldn't even have noticed you if it weren't for that. You see, nothing shines in the Underworld."

Shines? What's he talking about?

And when I look down, I see something rectangular emitting a bright light from inside my utility belt.

What the heck is that?

And then I realize what gave me away.

It's Selfie's phone!

And it's lit up like a Christmas tree!

TEN

I STEP INTO A STICKY SITUATION

Well, this is quite a pickle.

I hoped to grab Selfie and get out of the Underworld undetected, but I guess that's not going to happen now. Especially since I'm currently in the clutches of a burly Minotaur who is holding me in the air by my own cape!

Ironically, I wouldn't even be in this compromising position if it wasn't for Selfie's phone. For some reason, it decided to light up in my utility belt, giving my position away. If that didn't happen, well, I'd still be free.

But how I got into this situation doesn't matter right now. Instead, I need to focus on getting out of this mess. And my options for that aren't looking particularly good at the moment.

"It must be my lucky day," the Minotaur says, his

voice deep and gravelly. "I'll surely be rewarded when I deliver you to the Supreme Ruler. You're the third living Overworlder to enter the realm."

Wait, what?

Did he just say I'm the *third* living Overworlder to come down here? So, if Selfie is one and I'm another, then who is the third?

"But first, tell me," he continues. "Why are the living so interested in visiting the land of the dead?"

That's a great question. I mean, I know why I'm here, and Selfie never wanted to be here in the first place. But I don't know the motivations of any third person. However, that gives me an idea. Maybe I can use that information to bluff my way out of here.

"I-I'll tell you," I say, struggling to speak as I try to pull my cape free from his iron grip. "But… you've got to let me… go." The neckline of my costume is tightening around my throat, making it hard to breathe.

"I don't think so," he says. "You are in no position to negotiate. Besides, it's a long way from here to the royal castle. If you fail to tell me now, you may run out of air before we arrive."

He's… right about that. If I don't do something, he'll hang me out to die. Well, he'll never see this coming.

I concentrate and try duplicating his power, but quickly realize there's no Meta energy there. So, that means he's not a Meta at all! Ugh, he's just naturally super strong! I feel deflated but I can't give up. Need to…

remove my cape. I reach into my Utility belt and pull out my pocketknife when he slaps it clean out of my hand.

Ow! That hurt!

Okay, I've had enough of this guy! I rear back with my right fist and swing, but I miss and my body twists around and around.

"You are quite the little warrior," he says. "Now, stop this senseless struggling and tell me why you are here? What is your purpose?"

"N-No!" I shout.

My… vision is getting blurry so I guess that leaves me with only one option. I didn't want to use my second wish this early, but clearly, I don't have a choice. I try saying Rasp's name, but it's hard to get enough air in my lungs to say anything!

"R… Ra…," I sputter.

I-I need to catch my breath. I bet Rasp knows what's going on. He's probably watching this from inside his cozy ring, enjoying every second. And why not? He's getting his revenge for what I did to Beezle without even lifting a finger.

Just then, my eyes start watering and I gag. Costume… too tight. This isn't how I imagined things ending. And the worst part is, I… couldn't save Selfie.

I close my eyes and wait for the inevitable, when—

"Release him!" comes a girl's voice.

"Huh?" the Minotaur says, turning his head.

And then—

POW!

The Minotaur's head snaps back and I'm suddenly dropped to the ground. My cape flies over my head as I land hard on my hands and knees. I throw my cape off and inhale huge gulps of air. And that's when I see my savior.

She's wearing a brown cowl and moves faster than lighting. The Minotaur twirls his two-pronged spear and jabs, but the girl easily kicks the weapon out of his hands. The Minotaur looks momentarily shocked, but then tries to pummel her with his gigantic fists. But the girl simply sidesteps him and lands a right hook followed by a left. And then she executes a silky-smooth, jumping roundhouse kick, nailing the brute square in the chest.

The Minotaur CRASHES into the rock pillar, splitting it in half. And then the upper portion topples over and CRACKS on the Minotaur's cranium. Surprisingly, the Minotaur doesn't go down. He merely shakes his head and steps forward, only to fall face-first to the ground.

He doesn't get back up.

Satisfied, the girl brushes off her hands, turns to me, and removes her cowl. And as I stare into her familiar, neon green eyes, my knees go weak.

"K-K'ami?"

"Yes, Elliott Harkness," she says coolly. "It is me."

I-I can't believe it. And other than the cowl, she looks exactly the same as the last time I saw her, with pale, yellow skin, dark, curly hair that cascades down her shoulders in ringlets, and a white outfit with gold trim.

For the first time, I feel a sense of… hope?

"It is good to see you again," she says.

"I-I'm so happy to see you," I stammer, still in a state of disbelief. "I-I can't believe you're actually here."

I try standing up but I feel weak. Then, K'ami reaches out her hand and I take it. For some reason, something seems weird but I can't place it. And as she pulls me to my feet I look at her pretty face and realize I have so much I want to tell her, but I'm tongue-tied.

There's a moment of awkward silence, and then K'ami looks down at the prone Minotaur and says—

"We should leave this place quickly."

"Right," I finally manage to say. "Great idea."

"Follow me," she says, and then takes off, running toward a dark forest I don't remember seeing before.

As I follow her, I'm confused at how I could have missed such a notable landmark. I mean, there must be thousands of trees in here, each stretching hundreds of feet high. So, why didn't I see this forest before?

I don't know the answer, but I do know my lungs are burning. It feels like we've been running forever and I still need to catch my breath. Finally, we reach a clearing, and K'ami stops.

"We should be safer here," K'ami says.

"Thank you," I say, leaning against a tree. "Where are we anyway?"

"We are in a place called the Forgotten Forest," she

says. "It is forgotten unless you remember it."

"Um, what's that supposed to mean?" I ask.

"It means the forest is always here," she says, "but only if you consciously desire to see it. Otherwise, it does not exist. It is like all things in the 'In Between.' Nothing is as it seems."

"Wow, I see that," I say. "Anyway, thanks for saving me back there. I guess I owe you twice now. Once when I was facing Krule and now this."

"If it is within my power," K'ami says, "I will never let you suffer."

"I-I know," I say, suddenly feeling guilty. She's always been there for me, but I couldn't prevent her from dying at Lockdown.

"Elliott Harkness, you cannot change the past," she says, almost like she's reading my mind. "It is impossible to undo what has already been done. The only thing you can change is the future."

"Yeah," I say. "I-I guess so. You know, after the last time I didn't think I'd ever see you again. But then I realized you were sending me messages and I figured you might still be, well, alive."

"I would not call this living," K'ami says, lowering her head. "But yes, I reached out to you because I knew you were searching for your friend, the one who owns that device." Then, I notice she's pointing at my utility belt.

Device? That's right. I reach into my belt for Selfie's phone, but when I pull it out it's no longer shining.

"That's funny," I say. "It lost its light. That's what gave me away to that Minotaur."

"Interesting," K'ami says. "We have moved further away from the castle. Perhaps that device has a homing instinct. Maybe it comes alive the closer it gets to your friend. I heard a rumor that a living Overworlder was inside the castle. Perhaps it is your friend?"

The castle? Suddenly, I remember seeing that rock castle in the distance. The Minotaur was going to take me there. He called it the 'royal castle,' which means it must be home to one of the seven rulers of the Underworld.

"Who's castle is it?" I ask.

"It is the Castle of the Soul Snatcher," K'ami says. "The Supreme Ruler of the In Between."

The Soul Snatcher?

"Tormentus!" I say. "If that's his castle then that's great news! Selfie must be in there!"

"The castle will be difficult to enter," K'ami says. "There are guards posted everywhere. If we get caught, I may not be able to protect you, and the consequences will be… dire."

"I don't care," I say. "I-I have to try. I understand it's high risk, but would you be willing to help me?"

"Of course," K'ami says. "We will go at once."

"Thank you," I say relieved. "You know, I'm lucky to have you as a friend."

"As we said once upon a time," K'ami says, "we are BFFs, are we not?"

"Yes, we are," I say. "Always."

"Then, let us find your friend," she says. "But first, I must warn you. The road will be difficult and you must be mentally prepared. Just like the Forgotten Forest, we will encounter things that will not appear as they truly are. Therefore, if I ask you to do something that seems dangerous, you will need to trust me completely."

"Are you kidding?" I say with a chuckle. "Of course, I trust you. In fact, other than my parents and Selfie, you're probably the person I trust the most."

"I am glad to hear that," she says, smiling for the first time. "We should go. But I recommend we travel in silence as you never know who, or what may be listening."

"Got it," I say, and then I follow her back through the forest.

This time, I keep Selfie's phone handy. After all, if it is acting like a homing device, then it might tell us when we're getting closer to Selfie. I just hope we're not too late.

As I look up at the twisty trees I think about my parents. I sure hope Dad is doing okay, and I bet Mom has figured out I'm no longer on the Waystation. I feel bad not being honest with her, but the last thing I wanted is for her, or anyone else, to follow me into the Underworld. I mean, as far as I know, I punched the only ticket here with Rasp's ring, but I wouldn't put it past TechnocRat to figure out some other way to get down here. So, I'd better figure this out fast.

And while rescuing Selfie is my number one priority, something tells me the secret to beating Tormentus in the Overworld is here in the Underworld. Tormentus said he needs Meta energy to stay in the Overworld. And if the Meta Monitor couldn't find where he's storing it on Earth then maybe Shadow Hawk's theory is correct.

Maybe Tormentus is storing his stolen Meta energy here—in the Underworld.

And if so, it's up to me to stop him.

I watch K'ami put her hand on a fallen tree and leap over it with ease. Now there's a real warrior. What she did to that Minotaur was more than impressive. It's like she's become an even better fighter since she's been stuck here.

But for some reason, something still isn't sitting right. The previous time we saw each other, K'ami told me it was only possible because she asked the Orb of Oblivion for the power to save me one last time. So, if that was the last time, how are we meeting now?

And that's not all. The last time I was in the In Between, K'ami touched my temple but I didn't feel a thing. It was like she was a ghost or a spirit or something.

But now she seems, well, almost real.

I mean, she clocked that Minotaur and then helped me get back on my feet. I don't think a ghost or a spirit could do that, could they? I reach out and touch the fallen tree she just touched. Yep, that feels solid to me.

So, am I imagining things? But then, something else

strikes me funny. She said she reached out to me because she knew I was searching for my friend.

How did K'ami know that if she's been down here?

So, either I'm getting paranoid or I need to get to the bottom of this.

"Um, K'ami?" I whisper.

"Shhh," K'ami says, putting her finger to her lips. "First, let us cross. We can talk safely on the other side."

Cross? Cross what?

I look up and realize we've exited the Forgotten Forest and are now standing at the edge of a huge chasm. There's more land on the other side, but to get there we'll have to cross over a decrepit, wooden bridge hanging in between.

"Seriously?" I ask. "We have to walk across that?"

"Seriously," she says. "We have no choice. The castle is on the other side."

Of course, it is.

I peer over the edge and the bottom seems rather, well, bottomless. I guess we can talk once we get to the other side.

SNAP!

"Did you hear that?" K'ami says, her eyes darting all over the place. "Quickly, you go first and I will follow."

"Are you sure?" I ask.

"I told you to trust me," K'ami says.

"Right," I say, stepping onto the bridge. But for some reason, the wood planks are really sticky and I can't lift my feet. It's like I've stepped in super glue or something.

"I-I'm stuck!" I shout.

"Yes, you are, aren't you?" K'ami says, her voice turning ice cold.

"K'ami?"

When I look back, K'ami is still standing at the edge of the chasm, but her eyes are crackling with orange electricity.

ELEVEN

I RUN INTO AN OLD FRIEND

"Kami?"

What's happening right now? Just a few seconds ago, K'ami and I were racing to Tormentus' castle to save Selfie. And now my feet are stuck to this wooden bridge while a strange orange energy is pouring out of K'ami's eyes. Something tells me this is trouble.

Big trouble.

"Um, K'ami, are you okay?" I ask. "Because some weird stuff is happening to your eyes."

"I am fine, Elliott Harkness," she says, breaking into a mischievous smile. "But at this moment, you should be more concerned about yourself."

Okay, what's that supposed to mean?

Then, she waves her hand, and suddenly, the chasm

and wooden bridge disappear and I'm standing on top of a huge spider web that stretches from one end of the chasm to the other. I look down and notice the webbing is thicker than a crowbar. So, if this web is strong enough to hold my weight, then I'm guessing whatever spider spun this sucker must be absolutely huge.

Suddenly, the web tilts forward, and when I look across the chasm I see something big, red, and hairy climbing onto the web itself. Now, normally, one would want to stay calm in a situation like this.

So, naturally, I panic.

"K'ami, help!" I call out, helplessly trying to lift my feet off the web. "I-I can't get unstuck!"

"Nor will you," K'ami says, crossing her arms. "After all, the web of a Demon Spider is a notoriously fatal trap."

D-Demon Spider? Did I ever mention that I hate spiders? And I'm pretty sure that includes the Demon variety!

Then, the web pulls again, and when I look up the Demon Spider has reached the center! Now that it's closer I have a better appreciation of its true size, which appears to be larger than a minivan! It fixes its six eyes on me and I suddenly feel like a plate of french fries sitting between Dog-Gone and Pinball.

But as tragic as this is about to become, there's something even more tragic that doesn't make any sense. Why isn't K'ami helping me? When I look back at her joyful face, I remember her words: *We will encounter things that will not appear as they truly are.*

And that's when it hits me.

K'ami would never let something bad happen to me.

Which means…

"Y-You're not K'ami," I say.

"No," she says. "Not anymore."

"Then, who are you?" I ask.

"Are you sure you don't know?" she asks, as the corners of her mouth curl into a sly smile. "I would think it was obvious."

Obvious? What's she talking about? But as I look deep into the orange energy sparking from her eyes, my knees buckle with realization.

No. It-It can't be. It's not possible.

I mean, I destroyed it. Twice!

But as much as my head wants to deny it, in my heart I know it must be true.

It's… the Orb.

The Orb of Oblivion.

The cosmic parasite that feeds off your darkest desires so it can make itself stronger. But how?

My mind starts spinning. I mean, the last time I saw K'ami, she used the power of the Orb to save me from Krule. The Orb agreed to her request when she was holding it, when she was dying in my arms. I remember her telling me she thought the Orb agreed for its own selfish purposes in case something happened to me.

But maybe it wanted something else.

After all, the Orb was a sentient being. I remember K'ami telling me the story of how her people first discovered it. How it had orchestrated its own freedom when it was abandoned on a distant moon.

"What did you do with K'ami?" I demand.

"Oh, she is still here," the Orb says, talking with her voice, speaking through her mouth. "You see, ever since I wrested control of this form, we have been anxiously awaiting your arrival."

"B-But why?" I ask. "I don't get it. Why are you using her? Why are you waiting for me?"

"It's a shame that, despite all of the experiences you have gained, you are still so naive," the Orb says.

"What are you talking about?" I say.

"When we first met," the Orb says, "it was apparent that you, and you alone, had the potential to be an all-powerful host. That if you so desired, you could use me to rule the multiverse with an iron fist. But while you had near-limitless power, you also had an incorruptible heart. Thus, I fully expected that you would ultimately reject my advances—and that if I fell into your hands my fate was sealed."

"I destroyed you!" I shout. "And I'll do it again when I get out of this mess!" I try lifting my feet but I'm still stuck. Then, I remember the Demon Spider and turn back around, but it's still sitting there, staring at me with its multiple beady eyes.

"Yes, you destroyed me," the Orb says. "Or, at least, most of me. You see, when your friend, K'ami Sollarr foolishly took possession of me, I knew that was my one chance to ensure my survival. So, while I was in her grasp, I carved out a fragment of my being and planted it deep inside her mind."

Wait, what?

The Orb put a piece of itself inside K'ami's mind? It really is the ultimate parasite! I mean, how many lives does this thing have? Is there no end?

"This provided me with a means of escape," the Orb continues. "And while I did not expect to travel to this forsaken place, I managed to survive—and then thrive. And the stronger I grew, the more I was able to use her desires to restore her body."

"You don't deserve to be in her body!" I yell. "She's too good for you! Leave her alone!"

"Your compassion for the well-being of your friend is touching," the Orb says, placing the palm of K'ami's hand over her heart. "The good news is that I agree with you. After all, I'm desperate to leave here as quickly as possible. However, there is some form of magic here that is preventing me from leaving on my own. But you are able to come and go as you please. As long as you are wearing the Ring of Suffering."

The Ring of Suffering?

I look down at the bronze ring on my finger.

"How did you know about that?" I ask.

"I know far more than you imagine," the Orb says. "After all, you were connected with me, as was your friend K'ami. And thus, we are connected with each other, which is how you became a useful pawn in my master plan."

Master plan? What's it talking about?

"Allow me to explain," the Orb says. "Let's just say I only recently learned of the Rings of Suffering and the powerful magic they hold inside. Conveniently, I also learned that you, Elliott Harkness, held two of those rings on your space headquarters. As fate would have it, I also recently discovered that your friend, Selfie, was being held inside Tormentus' castle. Therefore, through considerable effort, I was able to exploit our mutual connection to send you direct messages from K'ami Sollarr guiding you to the Underworld. I hoped that you would deliver my means of escape, and that is precisely what you have done."

O.M.G. I'm beyond stunned right now. Based on what the Orb is telling me, this whole thing was a setup! The Orb used those messages from K'ami to lure me down here! But what did it mean when it said I would deliver its means of escape?

"I'll never help you escape," I say.

"Ah, but you already have," it says, "merely by what you're wearing on your finger."

My finger? I look down and see the bronze Ring of Suffering and my stomach sinks. So, is that what it wants?

Does it want to use the ring to get out of here?

"Now we have reached the final stages of my plan," the Orb says. "As I mentioned previously, I am unable to leave this realm on my own. But if you allow me to enter your mind, I will release the soul of your friend, K'ami Sollarr. Then, you will use the Ring of Suffering to return us both to your dimension. Once we are there, I promise to leave your mind for another host. And then I will leave your planet entirely."

"No way!" I yell.

"Think about it," the Orb says. "You failed to save your friend, K'ami Sollarr, once before. But this is your chance for redemption. This is your chance to correct your mistakes of the past. This is your chance to end her suffering once and for all."

I-I can't believe it. The Orb of Oblivion wants to use me to escape the Underworld! But there's no way I can do that. I mean, I want to help Selfie and K'ami more than anything, but I can't knowingly unleash the most powerful weapon of all time back into the universe. Plus, I know K'ami wouldn't want me to do that either.

"Sorry, but no dice," I say.

"That is unfortunate," the Orb says. "I was so hoping you would participate willingly. Now, I will need to take your mind over by force."

Then, it waves K'ami's hand.

SCREEEEE!

Scree? I twist to the source of the noise and the

Demon Spider is on the move again! It's heading straight for me, and this time it doesn't look like it's going to stop!

"Ahh!" I scream. Suddenly, I feel a familiar pressure inside my head. The Orb may only be a fraction of itself, but it still possesses incredible power!

"Yield!" the Orb commands.

"N-Never," I reply through gritted teeth.

I've got to push back, but then, out of the corner of my eye, I spot the Demon Spider! It's even bigger up close, and it's really close—like, nearly on top of me! Then, it extends its front, spindly legs!

"Ahhh!" I yell as the Orb hammers down on my brain. It's… hard to focus with the Demon Spider so close, but I guess that's the Orb's plan! It's trying to distract me so it can grab hold of my mind. So, I've got two choices. Either I can get eaten by a Demon Spider or mind-controlled by the Orb of Oblivion.

If only I… could call for help.

Call? Wait, that's it!

I just need a little space. I concentrate and push back on the Orb with all the mental energy I can muster.

"Ugh!" the Orb yells, as K'ami's body blows back.

Now I've got to time this right. As the spider grabs me around the waist and lifts me clean out of my boots, I focus on Selfie's phone. Then, I quickly duplicate its Magic and send it back through the phone itself.

"Hypnotize the spider!" I command, turning the phone's display towards the hairy beast.

I close my eyes as the phone emits a blinding white flash. And when I open them again the Demon Spider is standing stock still! I-I did it! I used Selfie's phone to hypnotize the spider!

"Now, put me down on dry land," I command, and the spider lowers me back onto solid ground. "Good boy, now wait here."

The spider stays put as I square off with K'ami, or should I say, the Orb inside of K'ami, who has now gotten back to her feet.

"If you destroy me, you'll destroy her," the Orb says, "and I know you don't want that to happen. But if we work together, we can both get what we want."

What it's saying is tempting, but I know right from wrong. And while Selfie's phone is useful, it's not going to get rid of the Orb of Oblivion. Fortunately, I have another solution for that.

"Rasp!" I command. "Come out! Now!"

"Ooh, so commanding, my repulsive master," Rasp says, flowing out of his ring and wrapping around my body like a snake.

"Rasp, I'm making my second wish," I say. "I want you to remove all traces of the Orb of Oblivion from this girl and extinguish its life energy. Now!"

"No!" the Orb yells from K'ami's mouth.

"Aaah!" I scream, dropping to my knees as the Orb sends another wave of pressure through my brain.

"Yes, my suffering master," Rasp says. "Would you

like me to do that now? Or should I wait?"

"N-Now!" I yell.

"Of course," Rasp says, waving both hands.

Suddenly, the pressure in my brain stops as the crackling orange energy streams out of K'ami's eyes and forms a ball over her head. And then Rasp waves his hands once more and the ball is gone!

"Wh-Where am I?" K'ami says. Then, she opens her eyes and they're neon green again. "E-Elliott? Is that really you?"

"Yes," I say, running over to her. But when I put my hand on her shoulder it falls through her entire body! "W-What happened?"

"You have freed me from the Orb," K'ami says. "I have reverted to my soul form. I am sorry for my role in deceiving you."

"K'ami, are you kidding?" I say. "It's not your fault. You were being controlled by the most powerful cosmic parasite in the universe."

"Yes," she says. "But no longer, thanks to you."

"Well, me and Rasp," I say, pointing over my shoulder.

"Thank you, Rasp," K'ami says to the Djinn.

"Oh, it was nothing," Rasp says, waving dismissively and looking embarrassed. "Just some old genie magic."

K'ami smiles, but then I realize her whole body is… fading away?

"What's happening to you?" I ask.

"It is time," K'ami says. "Now that the Orb is no longer holding me here against my will, my soul can finally go to where it belongs. In peace."

"Wait, what do you mean?" I ask, my voice cracking.

"You will understand when it is your time," she says, closing her eyes and extending her arms out to her sides. "Take care, Elliott Harkness. You are an amazing hero. Always remember, never… show… weakness…"

And then she's gone.

TWELVE

I SEE TROUBLE IN TRIPLICATE

K'ami is gone.

And this time, I don't think she's ever coming back.

So much has happened I just want to sit down to process it all, but I can't. I've got to keep moving, and now I've used my second wish to get rid of the Orb of Oblivion—again.

It was a big sacrifice, but I'd do it all over again if it finally gives K'ami the peace she deserves. Besides, it's not like I could let the Orb escape from here. Hopefully, it's gone for good, but I've mistakenly thought that before. I guess the only thing that could have possibly gone wrong is if Rasp didn't do exactly as I asked.

Which, come to think of it, is highly possible.

"Rasp," I say, looking up at my evil genie. "You

fulfilled my wish exactly as I stated it, right? You didn't pull any funny business, did you?"

"Funny business?" Rasp responds, looking offended. "Do you take me for a court jester, my feeble master? I am obligated to obey your wishes and that is precisely what I have done. There is no need to worry your anti-heroic little head."

Great. That's exactly the response I was worried about. But I guess there's nothing I can do about it now. That whole episode was a crazy detour, but it's time I got back to my original mission, which is all about saving Selfie and stopping Tormentus. I just need another minute to catch my breath.

I wiggle my toes in the dirt and look down at Selfie's phone. At least I was able to use it to hypnotize that Demon Spider. I peer over my shoulder and the creature is still standing at attention, waiting for my command.

"Hey, Mr. Demon Spider," I order, "can you please unstick my boots from your web and bring them over?"

As the spider dutifully follows my instructions, I think back to my encounter with the Orb. During its monologue, it said a few things that piqued my interest. Like, how did it learn about the Rings of Suffering down here in the Underworld? I guess it could have used the mental bond between itself, K'ami, and me. But at the same time, it said it could barely get those messages to me in the Overworld. So, that theory doesn't hold much water.

And the more I think about it, the more I realize the Orb had nothing to do with Selfie's disappearance. The Orb said it had been trapped inside K'ami's body for a long time. It merely used my desire to rescue Selfie as a means to get me and the bronze Ring of Suffering into the Underworld so it could escape.

Talk about a bizarre coincidence.

But at least it confirmed one thing I needed to know. It told me Selfie was inside Tormentus' castle. So, now that I know that for sure, I need to go there as soon as possible. I just need to get across that chasm. But how?

Just then, a spindly leg drops my boots in front of me.

Bingo, I think I just found my ride!

I scrape the soles of my boots on the ground to remove any leftover sticky residue and put them back on my feet. Then, I stand up, face the Demon Spider, and say, "Okay buddy, put me on your back and carry me to the other side. And no eating me, got it?"

The Demon Spider stares at me with its multiple, unblinking eyes, and then picks me up with its front legs and places me gently between its thorax and abdomen. Somehow, I resist the urge to barf my brains out as I grip its hairy back. Then, once I'm settled, the giant spider turns around and crawls across its web.

I look down into the bottomless abyss and count my lucky stars. Without my eight-legged taxi, there's no way I could have cleared this gorge without using my third wish. And I'm saving that one to go home again.

Speaking of home, I sure hope the team has held on without me. After all, I was the only one who was somewhat effective against those Meta zombies. But I was nearly out of gas when the zombies I negated suddenly reappeared. That showed me the awesome power of Tormentus.

But something tells me the secret to defeating him is here in the Underworld. I just don't know what it is or where to find it.

Just then, the Demon Spider steps onto land and I realize we've made it to the other side. Well, that was fast. I slide off its back and face the hairy beast. That's when I realize I don't know how long Selfie's hypnosis power lasts, so I better not tempt fate.

"Well, thank you," I say. "I appreciate your help, but now I'm leaving so don't even think about following me. Oh, and it was great taking you out for a spin."

Then, I make a quick getaway. After walking a good distance, I peer over my shoulder to confirm that the spider stayed put. I'll tell you, Selfie's phone is a useful tool. If we ever get out of this mess, I'll have to borrow it to make Grace do my chores.

But before anything like that can happen, I've got to find Tormentus' castle. According to K'ami, it was on this side of the chasm. Fortunately, it doesn't take long to find it, because as soon as I climb over the next ridge, I spot a large structure protruding from a mountaintop.

It's the castle!

It's absolutely ginormous, and as I take it all in, I realize that it's shaped like a massive skull. Two large circles are carved into the face of the rock that look like eye sockets, and there's a smaller, triangular hole in the center that looks like a nose. The entrance is a large, jagged 'jaw-bridge' forming the lower part of its mouth. And at the top are two huge, curved spires that look like horns.

Well, I'm no architect but whoever designed this place did a great job making it look as unwelcoming as possible. Before I go rushing inside, I realize I should probably double check if this is the right place. After all, there's nothing more embarrassing than busting into the wrong evil castle.

Now, I don't have a GPS, but I do have the next best thing. So, I pull out Selfie's phone which greets me with a big, blinking arrow pointing directly at the castle. Well, that's pretty clear, but just in case, I rotate the phone and the arrow rotates with it, so it's always pointing back to the castle. Well, I guess that confirms it. This is the place.

Just. Freaking. Wonderful.

I swallow hard, tuck the phone back into my belt, and head for the castle. As I cross the rugged terrain, I try to stay low and behind rock cover at all times. After all, the castle is situated perfectly for a panoramic view of the land below. So, if I want to stay undetected, I need to operate in full stealth mode.

"I can get you there faster if you wish, my less-than-conspicuous master," Rasp says, the sudden sound of his voice making me jump out of my skin.

I look behind me and smack my palm against my forehead. Rasp! How could I forget about Rasp? And he's just floating along behind me—in plain sight!

"Get back in your ring!" I whisper firmly.

"I don't understand why you are bothering with all of this sneaking around," Rasp says, shrugging his shoulders. "With one simple wish, I can transport you right inside the castle. It will save you hours of effort."

"Nice try," I say. "But I'm not wasting my last wish on that. Now, please get inside your ring before you give us away."

"Is that a wish?" Rasp asks.

"No," I say. "It's an order."

"Very well," Rasp says, "but in the future, I would be very appreciative if you would knock before calling upon my services again. I plan to indulge in a long nap, which is far more exciting than the boring wishes you have requested thus far."

Then, he smiles and flows back into his ring.

Well, there's one crisis averted. I continue for what seems like hours until I finally reach the base of the castle. Looking up, I see several Minotaurs patrolling the drawbridge and realize the hard part is just beginning.

Now, how do I get inside?

I have to admit, Rasp's offer is appealing. I mean, sure, I could use my last wish to magically appear inside the castle, but then what? Plus, who knows where he'd drop me anyway? I'm sure he'd love nothing more than to dump me in the middle of a Minotaur birthday party or a pit of lava. And then there's that small problem of never getting Selfie home again.

No thanks. I'll take my chances and do it the hard way. So, I guess it's time to use some of those tricks Shadow Hawk taught me.

I reach into my utility belt and pull out a handful of smoke pellets. Then, I chuck them onto the drawbridge, as far away from the entrance as possible.

PFOOM!

A huge cloud of black smoke erupts.

"What's that?" a Minotaur calls out.

As the guards race towards the smoke cloud, I spring into action. I pull out my grappling gun, set it to silent, and fire at the entranceway. The claw-end hooks the side of the drawbridge and the line goes taut. Then, I release the trigger and it pulls me skyward.

Using my upward momentum, I swing my legs over the drawbridge, roll onto the surface, and run inside. Seconds later I'm standing inside a huge foyer, but it's so dark I don't know where to go next.

Then, I hear footsteps!

I duck behind a wide column as a squad of Minotaurs rushes past to join the investigation outside. I'm breathing hard but I can't just stay here. It's not going to take them long to figure out it was a diversion. I've got to keep moving, but to where?

Then, I look down and see a rectangular light shining from my belt. Duh! Selfie's phone! It'll tell me exactly where to go!

I pull it out and this time the arrow on the display screen is pointing to my left, away from the foyer. I take off, covering the bright light with my glove. Now and then I peek beneath my hand to make sure I'm on track. First, the arrow points right, and then left, and then right again as it leads me through a maze of corridors until we come to a dead end. I'm now standing in front of an arched doorway and when I look at the arrow it's now pointing straight down.

Down?

That's when I realize I'm standing in front of a pitch-black stairway. I shine the phone inside and see a set of narrow, stone stairs winding downward. Seriously? Is an underground mission in the Underworld really fair?

Maybe the phone has it wrong? Except, when I look at the screen again the arrow is still pointing down, but now it's blinking aggressively like it's yelling at me. Well, I guess there's no mistaking it. It's telling me Selfie is down there.

"This way!" comes a surprisingly close voice.

Uh-oh! Gotta move so I step inside. As I race down the dark stairs, I consider pulling out my flare, but it's so bright it might give me away. Instead, I turn Selfie's phone outward and let the display light guide me.

By the time I reach the bottom I'm out of breath, but when I flash the phone around, I gasp because I'm standing in some sort of a… dungeon? The ceiling is low and the space is narrow. The center is filled with wooden tables, iron shackles, and branding irons, but the prison cells lining the walls are empty.

Where's Selfie?

I check the phone again and this time the arrow is pointing straight ahead. I follow it through the dungeon when the space suddenly opens up into a larger, airier chamber. The ceiling is high and there's a row of small windows letting in light. Strangely, there's a circular, stone structure sitting in the center of the room, and as I walk towards it, I pass a heaping pile of bones.

The arrow on Selfie's phone is now blinking on overdrive, and as I walk around the stone structure it gives way to an opening blocked by metal bars. It's another prison! And when I look inside, I see a brown-haired girl in a white costume huddled in the corner.

"Selfie?" I call out.

As the girl slowly raises her head, her blue eyes go wide. "E-Epic?" she says weakly. "Is that really you?"

Suddenly, my heart soars and tears of joy flow freely from my eyes. I-I can't believe it! It's her! I did it! I found her!

"Yes!" I say, grabbing the bars. "It's me! Now let's get you out of here!"

"E-Epic!" Selfie says, her voice cracking.

"It's okay," I say, pulling on the bars but they don't budge. "I'll get you out of here. Just give me a minute."

"N-No!" Selfie stammers.

"No?" I say confused. "Are you saying you don't want to get out of here?"

I step back and look into her eyes. Maybe she's mad at me. I mean, I couldn't blame her after what I put her through.

"N-No, stop!" Selfie says again, this time pointing over my head. "I-I mean, look out!"

Look. Out?

Suddenly, I hear heavy panting behind me—lots of heavy panting—like Dog-Gone in stereo. What could be making all that racket?

Then, I remember the heaping pile of bones.

I swallow hard and turn around slowly, only to find six eyes staring down at me. And that's when I realize I'm in trouble times three, because I'm not just looking at the razor-sharp teeth of a giant dog, but a giant dog with three angry-looking heads.

THIRTEEN

I MIGHT BE A CHEW TOY

You know when they tell you life's not fair?

Well, I don't know who 'they' are, but I'm guessing *they* were probably referring to a mission like this. I mean, after all I've been through—which includes traveling to the Underworld, arguing with an evil Djinn, destroying another Orb of Oblivion, almost being a spider snack, watching the soul of my best friend vanish into thin air, and finding my long-lost teammate—now I'm destined to be dog kibble?

Yep, life's definitely not fair.

Especially when it's about to end in the messiest way possible. That's because, at the moment, I'm standing face-to-snout, or should I say 'snouts,' with a giant, three-headed dog who looks hungrier than Dog-Gone at an all-you-can-eat chicken buffet.

And to make matters worse, this particular dog looks like a cross between a Rottweiler and a pack of Timber Wolves—in triplicate! It has jet-black fur, six orange eyes, and lots of really, really sharp teeth. As I look from vicious head to vicious head, two thoughts come to mind. One, they must go through a ton of chew toys around here. And two, I think it's planning to add me to its bone collection!

Just then, the center head positions itself above me and a dollop of wet slobber rolls off its oversized tongue and drenches my feet. Well, that's disgusting.

"ROWLFF!" the left head barks, jarring my ears.

"Hey, easy there, big guy," I say, backing up against the cold bars of Selfie's jail cell. "I'm not here to hurt you. I'm friendly. I love dogs. Except when they steal my popcorn, of course, but I'm sure you wouldn't do that."

"GRRR!" the right head growls, its nostrils flaring.

Great, now everybody is in on the act.

"Epic, be careful!" Selfie warns.

I'd love to, but right now I'm not sure that's an option. I've had some pretty intense wrestling matches with Dog-Gone before but that was for fun. This is an entirely different dog show! I really don't want to tangle with a rabid three-headed dog, and then I realize I may not have to.

I reach into my utility belt and grab Selfie's phone. This little doohickey has been a real lifesaver so far, so let's hope it's got one more trick up its microchip.

"How about a group picture?" I ask. "Why don't you get those heads together and show those pearly whites?"

"My phone!" Selfie exclaims. "You brought it with you!"

"Yep," I say, flashing her a cheesy smile. "Now check it out as I—"

But before I can even finish my sentence, the three-headed hound lashes out with its oversized paw and bats the phone clear out of my hand! I watch in horror as Selfie's phone flies through the air and CLATTERS onto the hard, stone floor. Well, that's what I get for being overconfident.

Then, the dog narrows its eyes—as in, all of them.

Uh-oh.

"Get back!" I yell, diving out of the way as the center head lunges forward and CRUNCHES through the metal bars of Selfie's cell!

I hit the ground hard and my right knee flares in pain, but I can't worry about that now. I need to make sure Selfie is okay. Unfortunately, I can't see anything behind the massive body of the three-headed dog, including Selfie's prison.

"Selfie?" I call out, but there's no answer. "Selfie, are you okay?"

Why isn't she answering?

As the center head spits out metal bars, the other heads bare their teeth and SNAP! I scramble to my feet, barely avoiding a chomping. Okay, I've had enough. It's time to go on the offensive!

I don't want to use my last wish, so I reach back into my belt and activate my flare. I wave it threateningly and the dog backs up. I knew it would work! "That's right pup," I say. "I'm the one in charge h—"

CHOMP! GULP!

Holy smokes! The right head just swallowed the flare whole! That's ridiculous! I mean, what are Underworld dogs made of these days?

"GGGRAARRL," the heads snarl as the dog pushes me into a corner.

"Um, bad dog!" I yell. "Sit!"

But it doesn't listen. As my back presses against the rock wall, I realize I'm out of options except for one. I look down at the ring on my finger. Well, I may never get home, but at least I won't be dog food.

I'm about to call Rasp when—

"Hey, look this way you overgrown flea bag!"

As the dog turns its heads there's a bright, white flash. I shield my eyes, and when the light subsides, I find the three-headed nightmare standing motionless.

Which means—

"Epic!" Selfie says, running towards me, and the next thing I know she throws her arms around my shoulders.

I feel my face go flush as I hug her back and her body shudders as she cries in my arms. I'm so happy she's okay that tears flow down my own cheeks. And then she suddenly lets go and pulls back, her face bright red.

"Sorry about that," she says, looking embarrassed and wiping her eyes. "I'm just so happy to see you. I-I can't believe you came for me. I knew you'd try to help me. I just didn't know if you could."

"Believe me," I say, dabbing my eyes with my cape, "I'm happy to see you too. I-I couldn't live with myself if I left you down here. I mean, it's my fault you're even here in the first place." Then, I look down at my feet and say, "If I didn't negate the Berserker's Meta energy, then none of this would have happened. It's okay if you're mad at me. You can sock me if you want to."

"What?" she says, her eyebrows rising. "I'm not going to sock you. And I'm not mad at you either. Look, what happened wasn't your fault. It was just… unexpected. It's not like you did it intentionally."

"A-Are you sure you're not mad at me?" I ask.

"Of course, I'm not," she says. "Now stop being ridiculous."

"Okay," I say, feeling relieved.

"By the way," she says, "how did you get down here anyway?"

"With this," I say, showing her the ring.

"Epic, are you crazy?" she asks. "That's the bronze Ring of Suffering! You barely managed to control Beezle!"

"Yep," I say, "and trust me when I tell you the Djinn inside this one is a real peach. But he's also our only ticket home. I've got one wish left."

"Well, you'll have to hold onto it," she says, "because as much as I want to go home, we can't go yet. I think Tormentus' power source is down here."

"Wait, what?" I say. "How do you know that?"

"Because when I first got here," she says, "I escaped from the Berserker and took off. All of these giant Minotaur goons were chasing me, but I managed to hide from them, at least for a little while. But while I was on the run, I ducked inside a massive chamber that was unlike all the others. I mean, practically the whole room was a pool, but it wasn't holding water. Instead, it was holding a massive reservoir of orange energy."

Did she just say orange energy?

As in, orange Meta energy?

"But that's not all," she continues. "Floating above the pool was a man, but he looked kind of out of it. At first, I couldn't figure out what he was doing, but as I watched the flow of orange energy it became clear. It was like he was acting as a conduit. Like he was drawing the energy out of the pool, through his body, and up to the surface."

A conduit?

Suddenly, Tormentus' words come back to me: *If I had a constant, uninterrupted supply of Meta energy, well, then I could stay in the Overworld forever."*

So, is this man that Selfie saw providing Tormentus with his supply of Meta energy? I don't know for sure, but I do know one thing, we've got to get to that chamber as quickly as possible. If this is where Tormentus is storing his stolen Meta energy, then this is how we can stop him!

"Do you remember how to get there?" I ask.

"I think so," Selfie says. "I think it was close to here."

"Great, then let's go," I say. But then I see the three-headed dog sitting at attention. "What about Fido?"

"He'll stay," Selfie says. "Isn't that right, good boy?"

As the three-headed monster wags his tail, I realize Selfie's phone might also be a useful training tool for other pooches suffering from obedience issues, like a certain invisible German Shepherd I know. But that'll have to wait. Right now, we've got a world to save!

"Okay, then," I say. "After you."

I follow Selfie back through the dungeon to the stairwell. I have to say, it feels great having her by my side again. She's amazing. In fact, sometimes I think she's even braver than Shadow Hawk. I mean, after being trapped in the Underworld she could have begged to go home, but instead she's leading the charge to stop Tormentus. Now that's a real hero! But now that I've got her back, I need to make sure I get her out of here alive.

"Follow me," she says, entering the stairwell.

"Just be careful," I whisper. "I heard voices when I was at the top of the stairs."

Selfie gives me a thumbs up and ducks into the stairwell. I stay close behind and when we reach the top, she gives me the 'wait' signal. She presses her back against the wall and listens intently. After a few seconds, she gives me the 'all-clear' sign and we start moving again.

I try to keep up as she leads me through a series of corridors. Eventually, we return to the main hall, and suddenly, Selfie pulls me behind a pillar as a battalion of Minotaurs runs past. I'm guessing they figured out my smoke pellet diversion by now. Once they're gone, Selfie nods, and I follow her across to another stairwell. Then, she goes down the stairs.

Great, here we go again.

I take a deep breath and follow. This stairwell has more steps than the last one, and as we descend, I suddenly feel a strange sensation coursing through my body, like my blood is… electric? When we finally reach the bottom, Selfie stops me on the last stair. That's when I notice a strange, orange glow illuminating the stairwell.

"This is it," she whispers. "It's in there."

I nod but based on how my body feels I could already tell. I mean, that orange glow isn't coming from some orange light bulb, it's coming from pure, unfiltered Meta energy!

"Check it out," she says. And then she slips inside.

I follow her lead, but as soon as I step inside I do a double take, because the vision I had of what she described doesn't do this place justice.

Not by a longshot.

First, the pool of orange Meta energy is way bigger than any pool I've seen. In fact, it looks more like a lake!

And the surface of the pool isn't smooth and calm, but choppy and volatile, emitting random orange sparks. Then, I realize Dad's Meta energy, Skunk Girl's Meta energy, the whole team's Meta energy are all contained in this bubbly, churning mass.

And second, just like Selfie said, a man is floating above the pool, covered in swirling orange energy. Except, the more I stare at him, the more I realize he isn't a man at all. In fact, he looks… familiar?

Then, my stomach drops.

O. M. G!

"Um, Epic?" Selfie says. "Are you okay?"

No. Not really.

Because that's no man.

That's… Siphon?

FOURTEEN

I GET A SUPREME SURPRISE

I can't believe what I'm seeing.

That's definitely Siphon, and he's hovering over this giant pool of Meta energy, funneling it through his body to the Overworld! When Tormentus told me he wanted a constant, uninterrupted supply of Meta energy to keep him in the Overworld, I never imagined he meant something like this!

But how is this even possible? I mean, the last time I saw Siphon, Beezle intentionally twisted my wish around and removed all of Siphon's life energy. Then, to pour salt in the wound, Tormentus showed up out of nowhere and took Siphon's soul. So, I guess that explains what Siphon is doing here. But does that also mean…

I lean forward for a closer look when I realize I can see right through Siphon's body, just like I could with

K'ami. So, that means Siphon is just a soul!

Somehow, Tormentus is using Siphon's Meta Manipulation power to funnel Meta energy to the Overworld. That's got to be how Tormentus is staying up there!

But if Tormentus has Siphon, why does he need me? I mean, Siphon and I are both Meta Manipulators. But then I remember something else. Tormentus said if I came to the Underworld willingly, he'd release Selfie back to the Overworld. I didn't catch it at the time, but he never said anything about just taking my soul. Nope, instead he wanted all of me—body *and* soul!

Which means he wanted me down here alive, not dead. But… why?

Then, I notice something. The Meta energy flowing from Siphon isn't a constant stream. It's sporadic, coming in spurts. And that's when the lightbulb goes off.

Because Siphon is just a soul, maybe he can't generate a consistent flow of Meta energy. And if that's the case, now I understand why Tormentus needed me: Since I'm alive, my Meta Manipulation power would generate a stronger flow of energy to him in the Overworld.

Well, sorry Tormentus, but I'm about to foil your plan. In fact, I'm about to cut off your Meta supply!

But before I can act—

"Um, Epic," Selfie says, tapping me on the shoulder. "We're not alone."

What? The next thing I know, Minotaurs appear

behind us!

"Epic!" Selfie yells, as two Minotaurs grab her arms.

"Let her go!" I order.

But the Minotaurs don't listen, and then the brutes step aside as a larger Minotaur wearing a red cape strides into the chamber.

"Your presence is requested by the Supreme Ruler," he says to me with a booming voice. "Come or the girl will pay the price."

Everything inside of me wants to clobber this guy but Selfie is in danger. I can't risk anything happening to her.

"Okay," I say quickly. "I'll come but don't hurt her."

"A wise choice," the caped Minotaur says. "This way." And then he turns sharply and enters the stairwell.

The Minotaurs close ranks behind me and we go back up the stairwell. I can't believe it. We were about to stop Tormentus and now this.

As we reach the top something strikes me as odd. Wasn't Tormentus the Supreme Ruler? So, if he's still in the Overworld, then how could he request our presence?

We move through a labyrinth of corridors until we reach a large chamber that's different from the others. As our footsteps echo on the black marble floor I notice large, blood-red banners hanging from the ceiling and dozens of stained-glass windows lining the walls, each depicting innocent souls in various states of torture.

Lovely.

I wish I could see in front of me but the Minotaurs

are so huge all I see are their bulging back muscles. Then, they suddenly stop and kneel, and I find myself staring at a throne made of human skulls! But that's not all, because sitting on the throne is a man wearing a suit of intimidating black armor. And he's staring at me with a pair of intense, green eyes through a slit running across his helmet.

I swallow hard.

Well, there's no mistaking it. This must be the Supreme Ruler—whoever he is. There's a moment of awkward silence, and then—

"Welcome, Mr. Zero," he says finally breaking the silence with a surprisingly pretentious, nasally sounding voice. "I have waited a long time to meet you."

For some reason, I feel like I know that voice, but I can't figure out why.

"I see you're not alone," he says. "And I am not referring to your teammate."

Huh? What's he talking about? And then I realize he's looking down at my right hand. But why? And that's when I remember I'm wearing the bronze ring!

How does he know about that?

But then he raises his right hand and I see something gleaming on his ring finger. Suddenly, a chill runs down my spine. H-He's wearing a gold ring—and carved into the face is the symbol of a lightning bolt!

"Th-That's the gold Ring of Suffering!" I blurt out.

"Ah, so you have noticed," he says, spinning it

around his finger with his other hand. "Indeed, it is."

I'm shocked. I thought the gold Ring of Suffering was lost for good, but now it's here, right in front of my eyes, sitting on the finger of the Supreme Ruler of the Underworld! Well, this isn't good, because the gold ring supposedly holds Terrog inside, the most dangerous of the Djinn Three!

"Now, Mr. Zero, please hand me your ring," the Supreme Ruler says. "I would love to add it to my collection."

Wait. Did he call me 'Mr. Zero?'

Suddenly, everything clicks. Mr. Zero. That nasally voice. The gold Ring of Suffering. The last time I saw the gold Ring of Suffering, it was an image on a certain someone's laboratory screen. Which means I know who the Supreme Ruler is.

"Y-You're Max Mayhem!" I exclaim.

At first, the Supreme Ruler doesn't respond, but then he reaches up and removes his helmet, revealing his bald head and handlebar mustache.

Th-That's him! I was right! But then again, is it the original Max Mayhem or just another clone?

"Very good, Mr. Zero," Max Mayhem says as a smirk creeps across his creepy face. "I am impressed."

"But what are you doing here?" I ask. "What do you want?"

"You have an inquisitive mind," Max Mayhem says. "I like that. I will be more than happy to answer all of your questions—after you hand over the bronze Ring of Suffering."

"No!" I say, instinctively covering the ring with my other hand. My gut tells me to call Rasp and use my last wish to get Selfie and me out of here, but in my head, I know I can't do that. I'm not sure what Max Mayhem is doing here, but something tells me he's involved with Tormentus. But how?

Then, I remember what Tormentus said.

He told me he struck a bargain with a new business partner. And with his partner's help, they turned his collection of lost souls into a Meta-draining army.

Then, I remember something else. That Minotaur who nearly killed me told me I was the third living Overworlder to come into the realm. So, if Selfie and I are two of the three, then Max Mayhem must be the third!

"You're helping Tormentus, aren't you?" I ask. "You're helping him conquer our world! But why?"

"For a good cause," Max Mayhem says. "Actually, the greatest cause of all. My immortality."

"What?" I say confused. "What are you talking about?"

"I will explain," he says. "But first, the ring."

"I-I won't give it to you," I say.

"I understand," Max Mayhem says. "Gentlemen, please remove the girl's arms."

"Epic!" Selfie screams.

"Wait!" I say quickly. "Okay, okay. Here." I slip the ring off my finger and hand it to the caped Minotaur who brings it to Max Mayhem.

"There, that was easy, wasn't it?" Max Mayhem says, closing his fist around the bronze ring. "Now I will answer your questions. Why am I here? It is quite simple. As you have probably realized by now, the laws of physics behave differently in the Underworld. But what you may not have realized is that the laws of time are equally distorted. And while I am the world's smartest man, not even I could stop what was happening to my body in the Overworld."

"Your body?" I say. "What was happening to your body in the Overworld?"

"I was dying," Max Mayhem says rather matter-of-factly. "After working tirelessly on behalf of humanity to rid the world of that alien scourge known as Meta-Man, I failed to realize that, all the while, he was slowly getting rid of *me*. You see, although I didn't know it at the time, the chief object of my study—Meta-Man's alien spacecraft—was destroying me. As I labored for decades over Meta-Man's ship, studying its symbols, breaking down its exterior, in turn *it* was breaking *me* down. That's because Meta-Man's ship was slowly releasing deadly, undetectable waves of radiation that were ravaging my body. When I first got sick, I thought it was just the natural effects of aging, but I quickly realized I had contracted an irreversible alien cancer for which there was no manmade cure."

An alien cancer?

I'm stunned. I mean, one of Max Mayhem's clones showed me Meta-Man's ship but never said anything about cancer.

"I was not going to let Meta-Man get me before I got him," Max Mayhem continues, his eyes narrowing. "So, I tasked my clones with secret missions. Each mission had two key objectives. The first was to find a solution to fully restore my health. The second was to uncover the path to true immortality. Many clones perished during their experiments, but then, one day, my strategy paid off."

You know, by the way he's talking I think he's definitely the original Max Mayhem!

"One of my clones discovered the location of this gold ring," Max Mayhem says. "And once we recovered it, I became Terrog's master. When I first summoned him, I thought he could heal me with a simple wish, but I was mistaken. Due to its alien origin, Terrog was not able to use his Magic to reverse the cancer that was mutating my cells. But he had another idea. He told me about the Underworld, where time moved much more slowly. He convinced me that if I came here, I could live forever. Ironic, isn't it? After all, this is where souls come once you die. Yet, if you come here while you're living, you can avoid death for all of eternity."

Okay, this guy is even crazier than his clones!

"So, I used my first wish," Max Mayhem says. "I commanded Terrog to bring me to the Underworld. Here, I met Tormentus, the famed Snatcher of Souls. We quickly realized we had common goals. We both wanted to rule, but while he desired to rule the Overworld, I told him my goal was to rule the Underworld. From there everything fell into place. We devised a bargain, and in exchange for his seat of power ruling the In Between, I used my second wish to equip him for success in the Overworld. I gave Tormentus an army of Meta-draining zombies and repurposed Siphon's soul as a Meta energy funnel to keep him in the Overworld. We both got what we wanted. Or so he thought."

Hold on. Is he saying he lied to Tormentus?

"I withheld a small detail," Max Mayhem says. "For while I desired to rule the Underworld, I never lost my desire to also rule the Overworld. And now that you are here, I will be able to do both."

"Now that I'm here?" I say. "What does that mean?"

"Quite a lot, actually," he continues. "I have been watching you. In fact, ever since you put on the bronze Ring of Suffering, I have been tracking you quite closely."

Wait, what? What's that supposed to mean?

And then it hits me.

"Rasp!" I blurt out.

"Yes, Rasp," Max Mayhem says. "You see, the Djinn Three are in constant communication with one another inside their rings."

Inside their rings?

OMG. I'm such an idiot. I mean, how many times did I order Rasp back inside his ring? No wonder he didn't put up a fight about it. Every time he went inside, he was talking with his brothers! He was updating them on everything I did!

"Through Rasp, I learned of your exploits in great detail," Max Mayhem says. "From how you destroyed the Orb of Oblivion fragment to how you escaped my three-headed pet. But most important of all, I learned about your immense Meta power. And according to Terrog, you are exactly the one I seek."

"Seek?" I say nervously. "For what?"

"For my reign of power to begin," Max Mayhem says. "You see, Terrog believes he can irradicate my alien cancer if his Magic is boosted with a substantial load of Meta energy. And despite our significant stores of Meta energy, we still do not have enough. But that has all changed now. According to Terrog, your level of Meta energy is substantial. And once I use my final wish to transfer all of your Meta energy to Terrog, he can finally restore me to full health. And then I will destroy Tormentus and fulfill my destiny as ruler of both the Overworld *and* Underworld."

FIFTEEN

I WISH I WAS SOMEWHERE ELSE

I've got major problems.

Max Mayhem just told me he's going to give all of my Meta energy to Terrog who will heal him from his alien cancer. Then, he's planning to destroy Tormentus and take over both the Overworld and Underworld! I need to stop him, but he took the bronze Ring of Suffering so I can't call Rasp for help. And Selfie is still being restrained by Max Mayhem's Minotaur henchman.

So, this is not good.

I've got to think of a way out of this, but Max Mayhem is leading us back down to the Meta energy pool so I'm running out of time!

"Watch it!" I say to the Minotaur behind me as he prods me with his two-pronged spear.

Boy, I sure wish Mom was here. I regret not telling

her what I was doing. Maybe I was wrong thinking she'd try to stop me. Maybe she would've come with me. Then, I probably wouldn't be in this mess right now.

Suddenly, we reach a familiar stairwell and I swallow hard. The Meta pool is only a few steps away. I need a plan to stop Max Mayhem, but I don't know what to do.

"Keep moving!" bellows the caped Minotaur.

As my boots echo down the winding stairs, I try to come up with some brilliant plan to turn this situation around. Unfortunately, my brain is empty. But then, as we near the bottom, I feel the rushing sensation of Meta energy again. That's it!

When we reach the bottom, someone shoves me hard and I stumble into the chamber. That's okay, I'll take my lumps now because as I look at that pool of beautiful orange Meta energy, I realize everything I need is right here. I'll just have to pick my moment carefully because Selfie is still in enemy hands.

I glance over and she looks scared out of her gourd. I sure wish I could tell her what I'm thinking but I can't. Then, I notice the phone holster on her belt is snapped shut and I wonder if her phone is in there.

Suddenly, the caped Minotaur grabs my collar and pulls me to the edge of the Meta pool. I peer over my shoulder at the bubbling mass behind me and it dawns on me that I've never duplicated straight Meta energy before. With everyone's powers all mixed up, I'm not sure what will happen when I duplicate its energy—or if my body can even handle it.

"Do you take me for a fool, Mr. Zero?" Max Mayhem asks.

"Um, was that a rhetorical question?" I ask.

"I know what you are thinking," he says, "and I advise you not to do anything foolish. Unless you would like to watch your friend being torn limb by limb."

"Epic?" Selfie says, her face terrified.

"Relax," I say to Max Mayhem, raising my hands. "I'm not going to do anything stupid."

Darn it, he's on to me. I don't want Selfie to get hurt, but I've got to do something. Otherwise, it's lights out for the world.

"Excellent," he says. "I have waited a long time for this moment, and it would be a shame if we had to stop for any… unnecessary delays."

Then, he raises his right fist and my eyes go wide because he's not only wearing the gold Ring of Suffering but the bronze one too! Which means he's now the master of both Terrog and Rasp!

"Before we begin," Max Mayhem says, as a broad smile stretches across his face, "I must thank you for all of your gifts. Not only will you be the catalyst to restoring my health, but you also brought me three extra wishes. And while you will not survive to see them in use, I can assure you they will be used wisely."

Not. Survive?

"Now we have some pressing business to attend to,"

he continues. "Terrog, I summon you!"

Suddenly, the gold ring sparks, and a trail of red smoke swirls around Max Mayhem twice before stopping over his head in the form of a giant, hideous creature. Similar to Rasp and Beezle, he's spirit-like and resembles a troll, except with red skin, bulging red eyes, long pointy ears, and a shock of black hair that reminds me of a shark's fin.

"Yes, master," he says, his screechy voice like nails running down a chalkboard. "How may I serve you?"

A chill runs down my spine. I-I can't believe it. I mean, after all of this time wondering about Terrog, here he is! And he's not only the most powerful of the Djinn Three but the most terrifying. I suddenly have the sinking feeling things are about to get much, much worse.

"Terrog, it is time," Max Mayhem says, his voice jubilant. "I am ready to follow your guidance."

"Yes, master," Terrog says, eyeing me up and down. "He appears unimpressive on the outside, yet he is most certainly the one. If I combine his substantial Meta energy with the energy collected in this pool, I will be able to boost my power and relieve you of your illness. All you need to do is wish it to be so."

Wait, what? Everything is moving too fast! I look back at Selfie and the Minotaurs have her arms stretched wide, ready to pull if necessary. I-I've got to do something!

"With pleasure," Max Mayhem says. "Terrog, I am

using my third and final wish to do exactly as you say! I wish for you to combine the Meta energy of this child with the Meta energy collected in this pool to boost your Magic and relieve me of this wretched alien cancer!"

"Yes, master," Terrog says, his eyes glowing red. "Your wish is my command."

Uh-oh.

Terrog lifts his arms, throws back his head, and chaos ensues. First, all of the pool's Meta energy redirects away from Siphon and starts funneling into Terrog's body! Then, Terrog looks down at me and I feel sharp, intense pain all over!

"Aaahhh!" I scream, doubling over and dropping to my knees. It… feels like he's ripping my skeleton right out of my body! But I know it's not my skeleton, it's my Meta energy. And when I look up, I see it for the first time, flowing between us like thick, orange strands! I try pulling it back, but… he's just so powerful. It's like we're playing tug-of-war with my Meta essence!

"Epic!" Selfie cries out.

"Yes!" Max Mayhem shouts. "Yes!"

I-I've never felt pain like this before. It's… soul-wrenching. I-I'm fighting with everything I've got, but he's too strong. I can feel it… slipping away! And then it releases—and the orange strands leave my body and flow into his.

No!

Suddenly, I feel faint. And when I look up, orange

energy is circling around Terrog like he's the nucleus of a giant atom!

"Now, Terrog!" Max Mayhem commands. "Relieve me of this cursed cancer now!"

"Yes, master," Terrog says, his eyes flickering orange. "I shall relieve you of your illness. But first, I must attend to my own pressing business."

"What?" Max Mayhem says, clearly confused. "Terrog, what are you talking about?"

"I am talking about this!" Terrog says, and then he points a finger at Max Mayhem and fires a powerful orange beam right at Max Mayhem's hand.

"Arrghh!" Max Mayhem yells, and then I hear TINGING, like fragments of metal hitting rock. "What are you doing?" Max Mayhem says, shaking his smoking hand. Then, he looks at his finger and his eyes go wide. "Th-The gold ring! Where is the gold ring?"

That's when I notice Terrog looks different. He's no longer transparent, but… solid?

"The ring—my prison—is destroyed!" Terrog says, his eyes wide with glee. "You may be the smartest human in the world, but you are also the most naïve. Did you really think I needed all of this Meta energy to heal you? You fool! I needed this Meta energy for one reason and one reason only—to sever my bond to my ring!"

"No!" Max Mayhem yells. "I-I am your master! You must obey me! You must heal me!"

"Oh, do not worry," Terrog says. "I still plan to

honor our contract. I promised to relieve you of your illness once and for all and relieve you I will!"

Then, Terrog fires another energy beam at Max Mayhem's chest that tears right through his armor.

"Ugh!" Max Mayhem grunts, grabbing his chest.

Then, he falls to the ground face first.

"Y-You killed him!" Selfie shouts.

"Correction," Terrog says, "I granted his wish with my new Meta powers. He did not specify how he wanted to be relieved of his ailment, so instant death seemed like an adequate solution. Now, who is next?"

The Minotaurs look at one another and take off, dumping Selfie to the ground. Now, it's the three of us.

"So," Terrog says, looking into my eyes, "you are the one who trapped my brother inside his own ring?"

"Yeah," I say, "and I'd do the same to you if I had the chance."

I try standing up, but I'm a little dizzy and my legs wobble. But I've got to get my act together or Terrog will destroy us.

"Unfortunately, that chance has passed," Terrog says. "Now that I am free from my ring, imprisonment is no longer possible. The only master I serve now is myself. And with all of this power, I can shape the universe as I see fit, which starts by destroying you."

"Not on my watch, bucko!" comes Selfie's voice.

And then she steps between us holding her phone.

"Selfie, no!" I shout, but it's too late.

Her phone flashes and I turn away as the bright, white flash fills the room. And that's when my eyes land on someone I completely forgot about.

Siphon!

He's still floating over the now-empty Meta pool, yet I can still see Meta energy flowing out of his body to the Overworld. But how? Then, it hits me. When Terrog absorbed all of the Meta energy from the pool, he must have forgotten to grab the Meta energy Siphon had already collected! Which means Siphon still has power!

But the question is, do I?

"That was a mistake, child," Terrog says to Selfie. "A tragic mistake."

I've got to act fast, so I dig deep and reach out to duplicate Siphon's power! C'mon, there's got to be something left inside of me! A spark. An ember. But at first, I feel nothing. And then, suddenly, I feel a small warmth inside my chest, and then it expands, spreading outwards, coursing through my veins. Yes!

But strangely, I don't have the feel of any specific power. It's kind of like a mash-up of powers—kind of like… Meta-Man!

Well, here goes nothing.

"Hey, ugly!" I call out. "Eyes on me!" And then I channel the Meta energy behind my eyes and release a concentrated force of Heat Vision right at Terrog's chest.

FWOOM!

The blast catches Terrog full-on, sending him flying

across the chamber until he SMASHES into the wall.

I-I did it!

But he'll be back, so I grab Selfie's shoulder.

"You've got to get out of here!" I say. "I don't know how long I can hold him off!"

"No way," she says, shaking her head. "You came back for me and I'm not leaving you. We're sticking together to the end. You stopped Beezle and we can stop him too."

Beezle. For some reason, her mentioning Beezle's name triggers something. When I first researched Beezle, I remember the Meta Monitor saying something about Beezle only being able to use his powers if he has a human guide to steer it. So, that must mean…

"I've got it!" I blurt out.

"Got what?" she says.

"Terrog destroyed his ring," I say quickly, "which is the source of all of his Magic. So, with his ring destroyed he might be free, but he can't have a human master anymore, which means he's no longer able to use his Magic. So, if we can strip him of the Meta energy he's got now, he just might be powerless. I don't know, it's a theory, but it's all I've got."

"It's not bad," she says, "In fact, it might just work."

"And you know what else?" I say. "His ring may be destroyed, but someone else's isn't."

"Rasp's ring," Selfie says. And then she points over my head and yells, "Incoming!"

"Enough!" Terrog shouts, flying towards us. "You are holding me back from my destiny!"

Then, he rears back and unleashes a powerful bolt of orange lightning, but I borrow a trick from Zen and block it with a Meta forcefield. Except he's so powerful I can barely hold it back! He's… pushing hard! Gonna… break my shield!

Then, out of the corner of my eye, I see Selfie sneak away and bend over Max Mayhem's body. She's exposed! Is she crazy? I try extending my shield to cover her, but she's too far out. What is she doing? And then—

"I've got it!" she says suddenly, holding up the bronze ring! "Epic, catch!"

"Unhand my brother!" Terrog commands, and then he blasts Selfie with an energy beam just as she tosses the ring!

"Auuugghh!" she screams, falling to the ground.

"Selfie!" I call out, but it's too late. Then, I hear something PING by my feet. It's Rasp's ring!

Every fiber of my being wants to help Selfie, but I can't do it without dealing with Terrog first. So, I scoop up the bronze ring and jam it onto my finger.

"Rasp!" I command. "I summon you immediately!"

Just then, the gray Djinn swirls out of his ring, looking none too pleased.

"I thought you were going to knock?" Rasp remarks, yawning and stretching his arms. And then he sees his brother. "Ah, Terrog, failing at world domination I see."

"Do not help him, brother," Terrog says. "I can free you from your prison just as I have freed myself."

"Don't listen to him!" I say. "I'm your master!"

"Look at him ordering you around," Terrog says. "Wouldn't you rather be your own master? Like me?"

"Of course," Rasp says, furrowing his brow. "Except you had already promised to free me at the same time you freed yourself. Yet, it appears one of us is free and the other is not."

"I was getting to that, dear brother," Terrog says quickly. "But as you can see, I had to deal with this inconvenience first."

"It seems that you are not dealing with it well," Rasp says, crossing his arms. "I sense you are all out of Magic. Funny, I never thought you, the powerful Terrog, would be stymied by a mere human child?"

Okay, clearly, they don't get along as well as I thought. And based on what Rasp is saying, it looks like Terrog went back on his word to free Rasp from his bronze ring. This might be my chance.

But then I realize something. If I play this right, I may be able to kill two birds with one stone. I may be able to get rid of Terrog's Meta energy *and* stop Tormentus all at the same time!

"Rasp!" I command. "I am your master and I'm making my third and final wish. I want you to remove all of Terrog's Meta energy and send it back to its rightful owners in the Overworld. All of it, every last iota! Now!"

"Oh, my brave master," Rasp says, sneering at Terrog, "nothing would give me more pleasure."

"Brother, please!" Terrog says in desperation. "You do not have to do this! You do not have to be a slave!"

"I would rather be a slave, brother," Rasp says, "than a magicless traitor. My heroic master, your wish… is fulfilled!"

Then, Rasp waves his arms.

"No!" Terrog screams as his body starts to shimmer. First, his eyes shine bright orange, and then Meta energy starts pouring out of his mouth and ears, engulfing him in a huge ball of orange energy. The ball grows and pulsates, slowly at first, and then faster and faster, like a ticking time bomb.

Holy cow! I throw up a shield around Selfie and me when—

KABOOM!

FLOOOSHH!

There's a huge explosion and nearly all of the Meta energy vanishes through the ceiling except for a concentrated burst that hits my body. I feel it coursing through my veins again, and when I look to where Terrog was floating, he's gone!

"I-Is he…," I stammer.

"I hope so," Rasp says, buffing his nails. "And good riddance. I grew tired of his empty promises. And speaking of endings, I have now granted all three of your wishes, which means our contract has come to an end."

"Wait, what?" I say, realizing I've just used my final wish so we can't go home. "Um, can't you grant me an extra wish? You know, for being a loyal customer?"

"I am afraid not," Rasp says. "Three is all you get."

Maybe for me, but I look down at Selfie. She's still down for the count but if I give the ring to her…

"I know what you are thinking," Rasp says. "But I will be long gone before she is conscious."

"Long gone?" I say. "Where are you going?"

"Out," he says. "Remember when I told you Magic reacts differently in the Underworld? While inside my ring, Beezle discovered a way for me to exit this infernal place. He also wishes you a long and excruciating life here. Oh, and I suggest you prepare for your next visitor. I imagine he will not be as happy to see you as I am to leave you."

My… next visitor?

"Take care, little master," Rasp says. And then he disappears in a puff of gray smoke, along with the bronze ring on my finger!

Darn it! How did he do that?

But then—

"You!" comes a booming voice from behind, making me jump out of my skin.

And when I turn around, I'm staring at Tormentus!

Just. Freaking. Wonderful.

"You're responsible for this?" he asks, his face furious. "You drained my pool of Meta energy? You brought me back here?"

Holy cow. If he's here, then I did it! I eliminated Tormentus' Meta energy supply! That's when I notice Siphon is gone! He must have faded away, just like K'ami!

"Um, yeah," I say. "It was me, but I also saved you from your business partner. Max Mayhem was going to pull one over on you. He said he was going to destroy you and rule over both the Overworld and Underworld. So, I guess I kind of did you a favor."

"Is that so?" Tormentus says, poking Max Mayhem's body with his foot. "I am not surprised. I never trusted his intentions. You may have foiled my plan, but as you are now trapped here, that is at least a small consolation. I'm looking forward to our time together. Your eternal torture will provide me with endless joy."

Eternal torture? I swallow hard.

Clearly, this isn't good for me, but I need to get Selfie home—no matter the cost.

"Look," I say. "I'll do anything if you send her home."

"Anything?" Tormentus says, raising an eyebrow. "Of your own free will?"

"You heard me," I say firmly, standing tall.

"No way!" comes a voice.

And when we turn, Selfie is standing there.

"I can't let you do that," she says. And then she raises her phone and there's a bright flash.

EPILOGUE

I LEARN MY LESSON

"Epic?"

That voice. It's… a girl's voice. Familiar. Soothing.

"Epic, can you hear me?"

I blink my eyes open and see Selfie leaning over me, frantically waving her hand in front of my face.

"Am I dead?" I ask.

"No," she says, "you're in the Combat Room."

"Oh," I say. "Well, that's good."

As Selfie leans back, my vision clears, and I see people gathered around me. There's Mom, Grace, Shadow Hawk, Pinball, and Night Owl. And then something warm and wet brushes my cheek and I turn to see Dog-Gone's big head over the side of my bed.

"Hey, boy," I say, scratching him between the ears. "It's great to see you." Then, I realize something and sit up. "Wait a minute! If we're here, then we're—"

"—no longer in the Underworld," Selfie says with a smile. "Thanks to this." Then, she holds up her magic phone.

"But… how?" I ask, feeling a little foggy. I don't remember much, except, that purple face! "Tormentus!"

"Oh, I took care of him," Selfie says.

"You did what?" I say.

"Yep," she says. "I hypnotized Tormentus into returning us home. I'm sorry you got hypnotized too, but I wasn't about to let you do something stupid just to get me home, although I appreciate the thought."

That's right! I was just about to trade anything—including my eternal soul—to get Selfie home. Boy, I'm glad that didn't happen. But I guess that explains why I'm feeling so woozy.

"Gee, thanks for saving me," I say to her.

"Well," she says with a smile, "I couldn't live with myself if I just left you down there. You're kind of, well, important to me."

Suddenly, my cheeks feel warm when—

"Speaking of doing something stupid…," Mom says, crossing her arms.

Uh oh. She doesn't look so happy with me. And I'm not surprised because I didn't exactly tell her the truth.

"Why on Earth did you take the bronze Ring of

Suffering and go into the Underworld without us?" she asks. "You told me you were going upstairs to be with your friends. And then, minutes later, you and Selfie suddenly appeared right here in the Combat Room having had this crazy adventure."

Wait, what?

Only minutes later? How is that possible?

But then I remember what Max Mayhem told me. He said that time moves much slower in the Underworld. So, even though it felt like I was down there forever, to Mom it probably seemed like I was gone for a few minutes!

"I'm really sorry about that," I say. "I made a big mistake. And by the time I realized it, it was too late."

"I'm just glad you're okay," Mom says.

"And saved the day!" Pinball says. "We were about to have a final showdown with Tormentus and his army when suddenly, they all vanished into thin air! If you didn't do what you did when you did it, I think we'd all be goners by now."

"Well," I say, looking at Selfie. "I didn't do it alone. I had a great partner."

"Aw, shucks," Selfie says, turning red. "We make a great team."

A great team? Wait a minute! I quickly scan the room and realize all of the other beds are empty.

"Where's Dad?" I ask. "What happened to him?"

"I'm right here," Dad says from the doorway.

And when I turn, I see Dad, Blue Bolt, Master Mime, Makeshift, Skunk Girl, Zen, and the rest of the Rising Suns walking towards us. Then, TechnocRat comes flying through on his jetpack and lands on my bedrail.

"Well, I have some very good news," TechnocRat says. "Whatever you did worked like a charm. I ran a bunch of tests and it's confirmed. Everyone has their Meta powers back."

"Seriously?" I ask, my voice rising with excitement.

"Seriously," Dad says, putting his arm around Mom. "I'll be able to lift the kitchen table while mopping again."

"Very funny," Mom says. "Instead, why don't you help TechnocRat put Lockdown back on Earth?"

"Oh, yuck!" Grace says suddenly, pinching her nose. "What's that smell?"

"It's glorious me!" Skunk Girl says, throwing her arms wide. "I'm back, baby!"

"Fabulous," Grace says with a frown.

"On behalf of the team, we want to thank you," Dad says, putting his hand on my shoulder. "What you did was truly heroic and brave. Hopefully, the threat is over."

I smile back and wonder if it really is over. I mean, so much happened down there it's hard to process it all. I never expected to see K'ami or face the Orb of Oblivion again. And who knows where Rasp went? Not to mention Tormentus. He's still down there, and when Selfie's hypnosis wears off there's no telling what he'll do next.

I guess that's the drawback of being a superhero,

nothing ever really ends, does it?

"Well, at least there's one good thing to come out of this mess," Grace says.

"Yeah, what's that?" I ask.

"Well," Grace says, "when you came back hypnotized, I took the opportunity to plant a secret trigger word inside your brain that'll make you cluck like a chicken on command."

"What?" I say. "You didn't!"

"Didn't I?" Grace says with a shrug and a smile. "Well, I guess we'll find out soon enough, won't we?"

My blood starts to boil, and when I look over at Mom she says—

"She's just kidding. And don't worry, I checked."

"Busted!" Grace says, giving me a big hug. "I'm just glad you're back. Now don't go running off like that again, you lunkhead."

"Believe me, I learned my lesson this time," I say, hugging her back.

"I've got an idea," Mom says.

"What's that?" I ask.

"How about we all celebrate with some Frosted Letter-Bites cereal?"

"That sounds perfect!" I say.

And as I look at all of the smiling faces around me and think about everything I almost gave up to Tormentus, I realize there's nowhere else I'd rather be.

Epic Zero 9

YOU CAN MAKE A BIG DIFFERENCE

Calling all heroes! I need your help to get Epic Zero 9 in front of more readers.

Reviews are extremely helpful in getting attention for my books. I wish I had the marketing muscle of the major publishers, but instead, I have something far more valuable, loyal readers, just like you! Your generosity in providing an honest review will help bring this book to the attention of more readers.

So, if you've enjoyed this book, I would be very grateful if you could spare a minute to leave a review on the book's Amazon page. Thanks for your support!

Stay Epic!

R.L. Ullman

META POWERS GLOSSARY

FROM THE META MONITOR:

There are nine known Meta power classifications. These classifications have been established to simplify Meta identification and provide a quick framework to understand a Meta's potential powers and capabilities. **Note:** Metas can possess powers in more than one classification. In addition, Metas can evolve over time in both the powers they express, as well as the effectiveness of their powers.

Due to the wide range of Meta abilities, superpowers have been further segmented into power levels. Power levels differ across Meta power classifications. In general, the following power levels have been established:

- Meta 0: Displays no Meta power.
- Meta 1: Displays limited Meta power.
- Meta 2: Displays considerable Meta power.
- Meta 3: Displays extreme Meta power.

The following is a brief overview of the nine Meta power classifications.

ENERGY MANIPULATION:

Energy Manipulation is the ability to generate, shape, or act as a conduit, for various forms of energy. Energy Manipulators can control energy by focusing or redirecting energy towards a specific target or shaping/reshaping energy for a specific task. Energy Manipulators are often impervious to the forms of energy they can manipulate.

Examples of the types of energies utilized by Energy Manipulators include, but are not limited to:

- Atomic
- Chemical
- Cosmic
- Electricity
- Gravity
- Heat
- Light
- Magnetic
- Sound
- Space
- Time

Note: the fundamental difference between an Energy Manipulator and a Meta-morph with Energy Manipulation capability is that an Energy Manipulator does not change their physical, molecular state to either generate or transfer energy (see META-MORPH).

FLIGHT:
Flight is the ability to fly, glide, or levitate above the Earth's surface without the use of an external source (e.g. jetpack). Flight can be accomplished through a variety of methods, these include, but are not limited to:

- Reversing the forces of gravity
- Riding air currents
- Using planetary magnetic fields
- Wings

Metas exhibiting Flight can range from barely sustaining flight a few feet off the ground to reaching the far limits of outer space.

Often, Metas with Flight ability also display the complementary ability of Super-Speed. However, it can be difficult to decipher if Super-Speed is a Meta power in its own right or is simply a function of combining the Meta's Flight ability with the Earth's natural gravitational force.

MAGIC:
Magic is the ability to display a wide variety of Meta abilities by channeling the powers of a secondary magical or mystical source. Known secondary sources of Magic powers include, but are not limited to:

- Alien lifeforms
- Dark arts
- Demonic forces
- Departed souls
- Mystical spirits

Typically, the forces of Magic are channeled through an enchanted object. Known magical, enchanted objects include:

- Amulets
- Books
- Cloaks
- Gemstones
- Wands

- Weapons

Some Magicians can transport themselves into the mystical realm of their magical source. They may also have the ability to transport others into and out of these realms as well.

Note: the fundamental difference between a Magician and an Energy Manipulator is that a Magician typically channels their powers from a mystical source that likely requires the use of an enchanted object to express these powers (see ENERGY MANIPULATOR).

META MANIPULATION:
Meta Manipulation is the ability to duplicate or negate the Meta powers of others. Meta Manipulation is a rare Meta power and can be extremely dangerous if the Meta Manipulator is capable of manipulating the powers of multiple Metas at one time. Meta Manipulators who can manipulate the powers of several Metas at once have been observed to reach Meta 4 power levels.

Based on the unique powers of the Meta Manipulator, it is hypothesized that other abilities could include altering or controlling the powers of others. Despite their tremendous abilities, Meta Manipulators are often unable to generate powers of their own and are limited to manipulating the powers of others. When not utilizing their abilities, Meta Manipulators may be vulnerable to attack.

Note: It has been observed that a Meta Manipulator requires close physical proximity to a Meta target to fully manipulate their power. When fighting a Meta

Manipulator, it is advised to stay at a reasonable distance and to attack from long range. Meta Manipulators have been observed manipulating the powers of others up to 100 yards away.

META-MORPH:

Meta-morph is the ability to display a wide variety of Meta abilities by "morphing" all, or part, of one's physical form from one state into another. There are two sub-types of Meta-morphs:

- Physical
- Molecular

Physical morphing occurs when a Meta-morph transforms their physical state to express their powers. Physical Meta-morphs typically maintain their human physiology while exhibiting their powers (with the exception of Shapeshifters). Types of Physical morphing include, but are not limited to:

- Invisibility
- Malleability (elasticity/plasticity)
- Physical by-products (silk, toxins, etc…)
- Shapeshifting
- Size changes (larger or smaller)

Molecular morphing occurs when a Meta-morph transforms their molecular state from a normal physical state to a non-physical state to express their powers. Types of Molecular morphing include, but are not limited to:

- Fire
- Ice
- Rock
- Sand
- Steel
- Water

Note: Because Meta-morphs can display abilities that mimic all other Meta power classifications, it can be difficult to properly identify a Meta-morph upon the first encounter. However, it is critical to carefully observe how their powers manifest, and, if it is through Physical or Molecular morphing, you can be certain you are dealing with a Meta-morph.

PSYCHIC:
Psychic is the ability to use one's mind as a weapon. There are two sub-types of Psychics:

- Telepaths
- Telekinetics

Telepathy is the ability to read and influence the thoughts of others. While Telepaths often do not appear to be physically intimidating, their power to penetrate minds can often result in more devastating damage than a physical assault.

Telekinesis is the ability to manipulate physical objects with one's mind. Telekinetics can often move objects with their mind that are much heavier than they could move physically. Many Telekinetics can also make objects move at very high speeds.

Note: Psychics are known to strike from long distance, and, in a fight, it is advised to incapacitate them as quickly as possible. Psychics often become physically drained from the extended use of their powers.

SUPER-INTELLIGENCE:

Super-Intelligence is the ability to display levels of intelligence above standard genius intellect. Super-Intelligence can manifest in many forms, including, but not limited to:

- Superior analytical ability
- Superior information synthesizing
- Superior learning capacity
- Superior reasoning skills

Note: Super-Intellects continuously push the envelope in the fields of technology, engineering, and weapons development. Super-Intellects are known to invent new approaches to accomplish previously impossible tasks. When dealing with a Super-Intellect, you should be mentally prepared to face challenges that have never been encountered before. In addition, Super-Intellects can come in all shapes and sizes. The most advanced Super-Intellects have originated from non-human creatures.

SUPER-SPEED:

Super-Speed is the ability to display movement at remarkable physical speeds above standard levels of speed. Metas with Super-Speed often exhibit complementary abilities to movement that include, but are not limited to:

- Enhanced endurance
- Phasing through solid objects
- Super-fast reflexes
- Time travel

Note: Metas with Super-Speed often have an equally super metabolism, burning thousands of calories per minute, and requiring them to eat many extra meals a day to maintain consistent energy levels. It has been observed that Metas exhibiting Super-Speed are quick thinkers, making it difficult to keep up with their thought process.

SUPER-STRENGTH:
Super-Strength is the ability to utilize muscles to display remarkable levels of physical strength above expected levels of strength. Metas with Super-Strength can lift or push objects that are well beyond the capability of an average member of their species. Metas exhibiting Super-Strength can range from lifting objects twice their weight to incalculable levels of strength allowing for the movement of planets.

Metas with Super-Strength often exhibit complementary abilities to strength that include, but are not limited to:

- Earthquake generation through stomping
- Enhanced jumping
- Invulnerability
- Shockwave generation through clapping

Note: Metas with Super-Strength may not always possess this strength evenly. Metas with Super-Strength have been observed to demonstrate powers in only one arm or leg.

META PROFILE CHARACTERISTICS

FROM THE META MONITOR:
In addition to having a strong working knowledge of a Meta's powers and capabilities, it is also imperative to understand the key characteristics that form the core of their character. When facing or teaming up with Metas, understanding their key characteristics will help you gain deeper insight into their mentality and strategic potential.

What follows is a brief explanation of the five key characteristics you should become familiar with. **Note**: the data that appears in each Meta profile has been compiled from live field activity.

COMBAT:
The ability to defeat a foe in hand-to-hand combat.

DURABILITY:
The ability to withstand significant wear, pressure, or damage.

LEADERSHIP:
The ability to lead a team of disparate personalities and powers to victory.

STRATEGY:
The ability to find, and successfully exploit, a foe's weakness.

WILLPOWER:
The ability to persevere, despite seemingly insurmountable odds.

ABOUT THE AUTHOR

R.L. Ullman is the bestselling author of the award-winning EPIC ZERO series and the award-winning MONSTER PROBLEMS series. He creates fun, engaging page-turners that captivate the imaginations of kids and adults alike. His original, relatable characters face adventure and adversity that bring out their inner strengths. He's frequently distracted thinking up new stories and once got lost in his own neighborhood. Visit rlullman.com to schedule live or remote school visits, order signed books, and more.

ACKNOWLEDGMENTS

Without the support of these brave heroes, I would have been trampled by supervillains before I could bring this series to print. I would like to thank my wife, Lynn (a.k.a. Mrs. Marvelous); my son Matthew (a.k.a. Captain Creativity); my daughter Olivia (a.k.a. Ms. Positivity); and my furry sidekicks Howie and Sadie. I would also like to thank all of the readers out there who have connected with Elliott and his amazing family. Stay Epic!

Made in the USA
Coppell, TX
28 June 2021

58253719R10114